CLUB
CSI:^{TM}

The Case of the Ruined Ram

by David Lewman

Simon Spotlight

New York   London   Toronto   Sydney   New Delhi

SIMON SPOTLIGHT

An imprint of Simon & Schuster Children's Publishing Division
1230 Avenue of the Americas, New York, New York 10020
© 2012 by CBS Broadcasting Inc. and Entertainment AB Funding LLC.
All Rights Reserved. CSI: CRIME SCENE INVESTIGATION in USA is a
trademark of CBS Broadcasting Inc. and outside USA is a trademark of
Entertainment AB Funding LLC.
All rights reserved, including the right of reproduction in whole or
in part in any form. SIMON SPOTLIGHT and colophon are registered
trademarks of Simon & Schuster, Inc. For information about special
discounts for bulk purchases, please contact Simon & Schuster
Special Sales at 1-866-506-1949 or business@simonandschuster.com.
Manufactured in the United States of America 0712 FFG
First Edition 10 9 8 7 6 5 4 3 2 1
ISBN 978-1-4424-3397-7 (pbk)
ISBN 978-1-4424-4672-4 (hc)
ISBN 978-1-4424-6690-6 (eBook)
Library of Congress Control Number 2012935962

On a cool Friday evening in fall, Corey, Ben, and Hannah hurried to the pep rally at Woodlands High School. It was the night before the big football game against the Rams' crosstown rivals, the Jefferson High Vikings. In this small Nevada town, the game between Woodlands and Jefferson was one of the biggest events of the year.

Hannah pulled her sweater tight around her to keep warm. "Why are we going to this pep rally, anyway?" she asked. "We're in middle school, not high school."

"And we don't care about football," Ben added. He was missing a really interesting show about black holes on the Science Channel. He wished his parents would get a DVR so he could record all his

favorite shows. But every time he mentioned it, they said a DVR was "unnecessary."

"*I* care about football!" Corey said. "I *play* football, remember? We may be in middle school right now, but in a couple of years we'll be in high school."

Ben stuck his hands into the pockets of his jacket. "Can't we just wait until then to go to the pep rallies?"

Corey raised both hands in disbelief. "No! By going now, we'll learn something about what it's like to go to high school. We'll be prepared."

This actually made some sense to Hannah. She'd found that the more you knew about something ahead of time, the less scary it was. In ballet, the more you rehearsed, the calmer you were during the recitals. "Okay," she said. "That sounds like a pretty good idea."

"Yeah," said Ben slowly. He turned to Corey. "But since when do you prepare for anything? Last summer you showed up at the pool without sunblock, money, or your bathing suit. We had to walk all the way back to your house."

Corey shrugged. "Maybe I've changed. Maybe

this is the new me. Prepared. Organized. Ready."

"Freezing," Hannah added, shivering.

"It's not that bad," Corey said. "But if you're cold, we can always walk faster. That'll warm us up."

Corey quickened his pace, and Ben and Hannah had to hurry to keep up with him.

When they reached the high school, a kid named Ethan recognized Corey. "Hey, dude! Here for the bonfire? Go, Rams!"

Ethan high-fived Corey and then disappeared into the crowd. Now Hannah understood why they were at the pep rally. "A bonfire, huh?" she said, smiling. "Suddenly it all makes sense."

"Right," Ben agreed. "There are three things Corey loves: bonfires, explosions, and bonfires that end in explosions." He and Hannah knew Corey pretty well. They'd been in school with him since kindergarten. The three classmates had even started their own club after they began taking a forensic science class with Miss Hodges. Club CSI had already solved three crimes.

Corey grinned. "Hey, the bonfire is a school tradition. And I hear it's pretty sweet. Although I don't think there'll be an explosion. Unfortunately."

The three friends wandered around the grounds of the high school. Lots of people were talking and laughing—mostly high school students. The Woodlands High School marching band was setting up, getting ready to play. Now and then a saxophone squeaked or a tuba blatted. And you could hear the drummers pretty much all the time. Once they strapped on their marching drums and got out their sticks, they couldn't resist playing.

"There it is!" Corey said, pointing toward a parking lot. He led Ben and Hannah over to the big pile of wood stacked carefully by members of the town's fire department. The fire officers were standing by their red truck, waiting to light the bonfire. They were also there to make sure it didn't get out of hand.

"The firefighters must be excited," Corey said. "This is the one time all year when they get to *light* a fire."

"Actually," Ben said, "firefighters often light backfires to keep forest fires from spreading—"

But Corey didn't hear him. He'd already walked

4

up to one of the firefighters. "Excuse me, sir," he asked. "When are you going to light the bonfire?"

The firefighter looked as though he were a little tired of being asked this question. "At the end of the pep rally," he said.

Corey looked disappointed. "Oh," he said. "I thought maybe the bonfire would be lit for the whole rally. To provide light."

"And warmth," Hannah added.

"Nope," the firefighter said.

"How long is the pep rally supposed to last?" Corey asked.

The firefighter shrugged.

They'd have to wait, and Corey wasn't exactly known for his patience. But to his relief, the pep rally soon got under way. Cheerleaders led the crowd in some rousing cheers. The band played a medley of pop songs. They hit a few wrong notes, but they were loud and enthusiastic. Especially the drummers.

"Where's the mascot?" Hannah asked. "Doesn't somebody dress up as a ram?"

She was right. Woodlands High School's beloved mascot was nowhere to be seen.

"That's weird," Ben said. "How can the mascot miss a pep rally?"

"Maybe he's busy being herded by a Border collie mascot," Corey joked.

"Or pulling his wool over someone's eyes," Ben added.

"Or helping someone fall asleep," Hannah suggested. They laughed at the idea of a sheep too busy to show up at a rally.

But a high school kid standing nearby, wearing a Rams sweatshirt, wasn't laughing. "It's typical," he said. "So typical."

"What is?" Corey asked.

"Mitchell not showing up," he replied.

"Who's Mitchell?" Hannah wondered.

The kid shook his head, looking disgusted. "Mitchell is the guy they picked to be Rocky the Ram, though I have no idea why. He's not committed to being the mascot."

"Being a mascot takes commitment?" Ben asked. "I thought you just put on the costume and then jumped around."

The fan looked offended. "There's a lot more to it than that!" he almost shouted. "You should

know the history of the mascot. You should have a signature move. You should be good at inspiring the crowd."

Corey was impressed. "Seems like you've given this mascot business a lot of thought. Maybe you should be Rocky the Ram."

"Thank you," he said, nodding vigorously. "Exactly. If I, Logan Canfield, was Rocky, there's no way I would've missed the rally for the game against the Vikings. It's the biggest game of the year! The mascot should know that! And be here!"

Logan stomped away.

"Logan Canfield is kind of intense," Hannah said.

"Not as intense as that guy," Corey said, pointing.

Hannah and Ben looked in the direction Corey was pointing. They saw a man on the edge of the rally holding up a sign. The letters on the white sign looked as though they had been neatly painted by hand. They spelled out GROW MINDS, NOT MUSCLES!

The man was rhythmically pumping his sign and chanting, "Grow minds, not muscles!" He tried to get people to join his chant, but no one did. In fact, people seemed to be avoiding him.

"Who is he?" Ben asked. A nearby girl overheard

him and laughed. "That's Mr. Powell, the old art teacher. He's retired, but he shows up at all the games and pep rallies to protest," she said.

"Protest what?" Hannah asked.

"He thinks the school district spends too much money on sports," the girl explained. "He thinks they should spend more on the arts."

"More money for the arts sounds good," Hannah said.

"But less money for sports sounds terrible," Corey added.

"I say more money for everyone," Ben concluded. "Especially us."

They decided to walk to the other side of the rally, away from Mr. Powell and his one-man protest. They could still hear him chanting as they walked away. "Grow minds, not muscles!"

Even without Rocky the Ram, the crowd was getting excited. One of the assistant coaches was talking into a megaphone, getting everyone charged up. Soon, the players would run out in their uniforms and everyone would cheer.

But Ben noticed a few guys who didn't seem excited at all. They hung back, watching the rally from behind a tree. "What's the deal with those guys over there? Behind the tree," he said. "Not much school spirit."

Hannah and Corey looked. "I think I recognize one of those guys," Corey said. "He plays football. A running back. Really fast."

"Why is he behind that tree?" Hannah wondered. "Shouldn't he be putting on his uniform?"

Corey shook his head. "He doesn't play for Woodlands. He goes to Jefferson. He's a Viking, not a Ram."

"Then what's he doing here?" Ben asked.

"Invading?" Corey suggested.

A big cheer went up. As the marching band played the school's fight song, the football players came running out of the gym wearing their uniforms. They ran across the football field toward the pep rally.

"Finally!" Corey said. "Now they can light the bonfire."

Not quite. First the coach had to thank everyone for the rally and to say a few words about what a good job the team was doing this year, and how hard they were working, and how they were one of the best teams it'd ever been his pleasure to coach, and how they were sure to win tomorrow. . . .

And then, at last, it was time for the bonfire.

The firefighters lit the pile of wood. The flames spread quickly, leaping into the dark sky. The fire crackled. The smell of burning wood filled the night air.

Corey watched the fire, smiling. It was even bigger than he'd imagined. Ben and Hannah enjoyed the bonfire too. "This was a good idea," Hannah said. "And I'm finally warm."

But after a few minutes, Corey turned to Ben and Hannah and said, "Okay, let's go."

"Already?" Hannah asked.

"But the fire's still burning," Ben said. "This is what we came to see!"

"I like to see the fire at its biggest," Corey explained. "Not when it's dying down and going out and smoldering. That's just depressing."

Corey headed home. Hannah and Ben looked at each other, shrugged, and followed him.

The bonfire shot sparks into the night sky.

Chapter 2

The remains of the fire weren't smoldering the next morning. The firefighters had made sure the bonfire was completely out before they left. All that remained were cold black cinders and gray ashes.

Two custodians from the high school trudged out to the parking lot to clean up the mess.

"Sure," one of them said to the other, "a bonfire's real fun. Unless you're the guys who have to clean up the mess afterward."

"It's not that bad," the other custodian answered. "We sweep up the ashes and hose off the parking lot. Simple."

"Well then," the first custodian said, snorting, "maybe I should just let you handle it by yourself."

Despite his grumbling, they both got right to work with their push brooms. The bonfire had left lots of gray ashes and black chunks of scorched wood. But soon they noticed something else in the pile.

Something furry.

"What is that?" the first custodian asked.

"I don't know," said the second custodian, peering at the hairy mess in the pile of ashes. "I hope some poor animal didn't wander into the fire last night."

"I don't think animals wander into big fires," the first custodian said. "They're not that dumb."

Using a broom, they fished out the strange object. They stared at it. Then the first custodian realized what it was.

"It's an animal, all right," he said. "It's Rocky the Ram."

Sure enough, it was the charred remains of the costume worn by the school mascot. They could see the ram's head and the furry ram's suit with hooves on the ends of the sleeves and the legs. How had the costume ended up in the bonfire?

The two custodians looked around, puzzled. The

second custodian noticed something white pinned to a nearby tree. "Looks like a note," he remarked.

He quickly walked over to the sycamore to read the note. It read, GET READY TO GO DOWN IN FLAMES! VIKINGS RULE!

"Vikings?" the custodian said. "That's the team over at Jefferson High School."

"What should we do with this?" the first custodian asked, the burned costume still hanging off his broom.

The second custodian stood there looking at the note, thinking. "I say we take the whole mess to the principal."

"Is he here? On a Saturday?"

"Probably. There's a football game this afternoon. He'll be here for that."

His coworker nodded. They dropped the scorched costume into a garbage bag, unpinned the note from the tree, and headed into the school.

That afternoon Corey was at the football game between Woodlands High School and Jefferson High School.

He was not enjoying it.

He loved football. He loved playing it, and he loved watching other people play it—on TV or live and in person. On a sunny afternoon in fall, there was nothing he liked better than being outside playing or watching football. But he did not enjoy watching the team he was rooting for lose.

And today the Woodlands High School Rams were losing. Big time. At the moment, the score was 56 to 13. And it was only the third quarter.

The Jefferson High Vikings seemed to be scoring almost every time they got their hands on the football. And almost every time the Woodlands High Rams got their hands on the ball, they lost it to the Vikings.

Corey tried to experience the game as something other than a depressing, humiliating defeat. He decided to see it as a learning opportunity. He concentrated on analyzing what the Rams were doing wrong and what the Vikings were doing right.

Other fans around him in the stands were grumbling.

"What is *wrong* with this team?" one man said with a growl.

"I'll tell you what's wrong," the man sitting next to him answered. "They should never have played without Rocky the Ram. That's bad luck."

"Where is Rocky, anyway?" the first man asked.

The second man shrugged. "I don't know. But wherever he is, he's having more fun than we are."

A man sitting in front of them twisted around to share his opinion. "It's got nothing to do with the mascot. The players just aren't any good this year. In fact, they stink."

"Hey!" the second man said. "Watch what you say. My son's on that team!"

The men started arguing about why the team was losing so badly, and the spectators around them joined in. Some thought it was the players' fault. Some thought it was the coach's. Others thought it was the plays they were running. It was the defense. It was the offense. It was both. . . .

It was a lot more fun to argue about why the team was losing than to watch them lose.

Corey started thinking about how different things would be once he joined the high school team. He'd start scoring, and they'd start winning. And keep winning. Maybe even a state championship.

He pictured himself running the length of the entire field, returning the ball from a kickoff to score a touchdown, dodging tacklers . . .

A cheer went up from the bleachers on the other side of the field. The Vikings had just scored another touchdown.

After the game, the principal of Woodlands High School had driven straight from the football field to the police station. He was actually glad he had an errand to run. He didn't like the idea of hanging around after the Rams' loss. Parents would just come up to him complaining and urging him to hire a new coach.

He liked the coach. He worked hard and seemed to really care about his players. He stressed the importance of getting good grades. And he was a good math teacher. It'd be awful to have to fire him just because he lost a few games. Or even a lot of games.

Inside the station, Principal Hall dropped a plastic bag onto the floor of Officer Inverno's office. Officer Inverno sniffed.

"What's in that?" he asked. "Smells like a brush fire."

"It's our mascot costume—Rocky the Ram," Principal Hall explained. "Somebody burned it in our bonfire at the pep rally last night."

The policeman opened the trash bag and took a look inside. "Yeah," he said. "It's pretty badly burned, but I recognize it."

"Whoever did it left this note," Principal Hall continued, handing Officer Inverno the note the custodians had found pinned to the tree.

"'Get ready to go down in flames,'" the policeman read. He looked up at the principal. "Did they?"

The principal sighed. "Yes. The Rams lost. The Vikings were just too tough for them."

Officer Inverno frowned. "I'm not sure this qualifies as a police matter. It's really more of a school prank."

"An expensive prank," Principal Hall said. "These mascot costumes aren't cheap. And our budget is already stretched to the breaking point as it is. Whoever did this shouldn't be allowed to get away with it."

Officer Inverno nodded, thinking. Then he got

an idea. "All right," he said, standing up. "Leave the evidence with me. I think I've got a good idea about how to handle this."

The principal smiled, relieved. He shook the policeman's hand. "Thanks," he said. "I appreciate it. Sorry to saddle you with this smoky-smelling mess."

"Oh, don't worry about that," Officer Inverno replied, grinning. "I'm not keeping this bag in my office any longer than I have to."

Principal Inverno stared at the trash bag his brother had just dropped onto a chair in his office. "It smells like smoke," Principal Inverno said. "I hope it doesn't set off the fire alarms." It was first thing Monday morning, and he really didn't want to start his week at Woodlands Junior High School with a fire drill.

Officer Inverno smiled. "It smells like smoke because it's got a burned mascot costume in it. Rocky the Ram."

Principal Inverno looked confused. "I think you've mixed up your mascots, bro. The Rams are the high school team, not the junior high. We're the Bobcats."

"I'm well aware of that," the policeman said. "I was hoping maybe you could help me find the culprit."

Now the principal looked even more confused. "Me? Shouldn't you handle this? Or if you're too busy, maybe one of your fellow officers?"

"We're *all* too busy," Officer Inverno said, sighing. "We're swamped. With lots of cases that are more important than a burned mascot costume."

Principal Inverno fiddled with a pen. "Okay, but why bring it to me? Why not the principal of the high school? Principal Hall. It's his mascot."

His brother smiled. "Because *you've* got a forensic class. I was thinking this little mystery would be the perfect project for Miss Hodges and her students. They've done a good job before with cases that originated here in your school."

"I believe it was Club CSI who solved those cases, not the whole class," Principal Inverno said.

"However you want to handle it, bro. You're the principal," Officer Inverno said as he left, grinning.

Miss Hodges was preparing the day's lesson in forensics when she thought she smelled something burning. Had someone lit one of the Bunsen burners in the lab? She hurried out of her tiny office into the classroom to find Principal Inverno holding a black trash bag in one hand and a piece of paper in the other.

"Hello, Principal Inverno," she said, a little puzzled. "Is that garbage for me?"

He set the bag on the floor of the classroom. "It's not garbage, though I'll admit it does smell pretty bad. Smoky, anyway."

He explained about the burned mascot costume, and how his brother the policeman had brought it by, thinking maybe the mystery would make a good project for her class.

"Now, I know you already have your lessons planned, so if you don't want to do this, I'll understand perfectly," he concluded. "Actually, I'll understand if you just don't want this smelly mess in your classroom."

Miss Hodges smiled. "I think it's a wonderful

idea. It'll fit perfectly with my upcoming lesson on the forensics of fire investigation. And the smell doesn't bother me. Visiting crime labs and morgues, I've smelled much worse."

The principal was relieved. "I wasn't sure whether you'd want this case to be handled by Club CSI or your whole class."

"Oh, I think it'll make a terrific project for the whole class," she said enthusiastically. "Thank you!"

"No, I thank *you*," Principal Inverno said as he left the classroom. "I'm very grateful to get Rocky the Ram out of my office."

Chapter 3

Hannah, Ben, and Corey walked down the hallway at Woodlands Junior High School. They were on their way to their favorite class, forensic science. The teacher, Miss Hodges, was also the faculty advisor for their extracurricular organization, Club CSI. The club hadn't had a case to work on for a while, so they were eager to take on something new.

"How was the big football game?" Hannah asked. She didn't really care much about sports, but she knew they were important to Corey.

Corey winced. "Terrible. Didn't you hear? We lost horribly to Jefferson. It was a slaughter."

"That's good," Ben said.

"What?!" Corey asked, outraged. "How can that

possibly be good? Are you a Vikings fan all of a sudden? Because that would be traitorous!"

Ben laughed. "No, I meant maybe it's good that the high school team is so bad. That way, when you get to high school, you can be the star of the team."

Corey looked confused. "Are you saying I could only be the star of a really bad team?"

"I think he's saying you could come in and turn the team around," Hannah said, trying to help. "Change them from losers into winners."

"Yeah, well, that's still a couple of years off," Corey said. "A lot can happen in two years. In fact, the Rams might get better by the end of this season."

"You think so?" Ben asked.

"Not really," Corey said gloomily.

"Was the mascot there?" Hannah asked.

"No," Corey said. "Rocky the Ram was nowhere to be seen. Some people think maybe he's been kidnapped. Or defected to another team."

Ben laughed again. "So, he found another team that calls itself the Rams but doesn't have a mascot?"

"Maybe," Corey said. He hadn't really thought about how ridiculous this theory was. He was just repeating what he'd heard.

"You know that the mascot isn't real, right?" Hannah asked. "That it's just a kid inside a costume?"

"Mitchell," Corey said.

"What?" Hannah asked.

"Mitchell," Corey repeated. "That's the name of the kid in the Rocky costume. At least, according to that other kid, Logan."

"Okay, what was the name of the retired art teacher?" Hannah quizzed him.

"Mr. Powell," Corey answered.

Ben was impressed. "You may repeat a lot of wild theories, but you've got an excellent memory for names."

"Thank you, what's-your-name," Corey said as they went into the forensic classroom. Miss Hodges liked to call it the lab, and so did the members of Club CSI. "Lab" sounded so much more official than "classroom."

Ben stopped and made a face. "Ew," he said. "What's that smell?"

"It smells kind of like the time I accidentally singed some of my hair with a straightener," Hannah said, wrinkling her nose.

Corey sniffed the air. "Maybe today we're going

to learn about the forensics of barbecuing. Which would be great, 'cause I'm starving."

Ben raised his eyebrows. "If that's barbecue, I sure don't want to taste it."

"Fine," Corey said. "More for me."

"Based on the evidence," Hannah said, "I don't think much of your working theory."

"'I don't think much of your working theory,'" someone said mockingly. It was Ricky Collins, a big kid who acted tough all the time. His friends laughed.

"Don't you dorks ever stop playing detective?" he said with a sneer.

Hannah wasn't afraid of Ricky. "Maybe you've forgotten that this is a class in forensic science," she said. "We're *supposed* to be thinking about evidence and theories."

"Not me," Ricky declared. "I'm thinking about girls." He winked at Hannah.

"Gross," she said as she walked past him to Club CSI's lab table.

Another girl in class, Jennifer, told Hannah quietly, "Don't mind Ricky. I think it's really cool that you and Ben and Corey have solved actual crimes."

"So do I," agreed another girl, Kayla. "Very cool."

"Thanks," Hannah said, smiling gratefully.

Ben noticed that Ricky overheard the girls' compliments and looked like he was frowning. Could it be that Ricky Collins was . . . *jealous*?

Miss Hodges walked briskly out of her tiny office into the classroom and wished her students a good morning. Once she had their attention, she made an announcement.

"Principal Inverno has asked this class to take on a very special assignment," she said. "Perhaps some of you have heard that the high school's mascot costume, Rocky the Ram, went missing over the weekend."

"Not just the costume," Corey volunteered. "Rocky wasn't at the bonfire Friday night or the game on Saturday."

"Actually, as it turns out," Miss Hodges continued, "Rocky *was* at the bonfire. In fact, he—or rather, the costume—was *in* the bonfire."

She lifted a black garbage bag and placed it onto the table in front of her. Then she opened the bag to let the class see the badly singed ram costume. A couple of kids gasped. Others said, "Ew!"

"Someone *burned* Rocky?" Corey said. "That's terrible!"

"Mm," Ricky said, licking his lips. "Lamb burgers." His friends laughed.

Miss Hodges frowned. "This isn't a joke. It's a serious act of vandalism—a real crime. And you're going to investigate it."

Ben smiled proudly. He was sure Miss Hodges was asking Club CSI to undertake a thorough investigation. "No problem, Miss Hodges," he said. "We'll get on it right away."

Miss Hodges smiled too. "Thank you, Ben, but what I meant was that everyone in this class is going to investigate the destruction of the mascot costume."

Ben looked surprised. Some of the other students seemed a little uncertain. "All of us?" Jennifer asked.

Miss Hodges nodded. "In groups. You're going to break into teams of two or three to investigate the crime, as well as this note left at the scene."

As she held up the note, Hannah, Corey, and Ben exchanged quick looks. They definitely planned to work together as a team.

"The members of the team who solve the crime

will get extra credit," the teacher continued. "And as an extra incentive, Principal Hall at the high school has added a prize for the winning team: VIP tickets to the rest of this season's football games."

Some of the students didn't seem at all interested in tickets to the high school football games. But several of the kids did perk up. They were very interested. Including Corey. And Ricky Collins, who also loved football.

"So let's start off," Miss Hodges said, "by forming into teams of two or three. Go on—get in your teams."

The members of Club CSI were already sitting together, so it was simple for them to form a team. They were a little surprised to find themselves competing with all the other students in the forensic class. They'd gotten used to solving school crimes on their own.

"My coach says competition is good," Corey said. "It makes you a better player."

"Don't tell me about competition," Hannah said. "There's nothing more competitive than ballet."

"Ballet?" Corey said in disbelief. "More competitive than professional sports? I don't think so."

"There are a lot more professional sports teams than professional ballet companies," Hannah argued. "The competition to become a professional ballet dancer is unbelievable."

"But pro sports—" Corey started to protest.

"Okay, okay," Ben said, holding up his hands. "Let's not compete over whose activity is more competitive. Besides, science is *way* more competitive."

A couple of Ricky's friends in the back of the class assumed he'd join them on a team. But to their surprise, Ricky walked over to Charlie, one of the smartest kids at Woodlands Junior High.

"Wanna be a team?" Ricky asked gruffly.

Charlie looked up at Ricky, surprised. He'd been too shy to approach any of the other students about forming a team. He didn't know much about Ricky Collins. But he did know Ricky seemed like the kind of kid you didn't say no to.

"Okay," Charlie said slowly. "Sure."

Ricky grinned. "All right!" He clapped Charlie on the back. "May the best team win! Our team! Ricky and . . . what's your name again?"

"Charlie."

"Ricky and Charlie! The winning team!"

Once everyone had formed into teams, Miss Hodges brought the class back to order. Ben noticed she'd put the black garbage bag and the note back in her office. He raised his hand.

"Yes, Ben?" Miss Hodges said.

"May we examine the burned costume and the note?" he asked.

Miss Hodges nodded. "Yes, in time. But not right away. First I want to teach you some of the basics of fire investigation. And I need to finish preparing that lesson, so it'll have to wait until tomorrow. Principal Inverno only brought the costume to me this morning."

"So the contest doesn't start until tomorrow?" Ricky asked.

"Well," she said, "an investigation actually starts the minute you hear about the case. You can start thinking about possible motives. Why would someone burn the Rocky costume?"

"Because they hate sheep?" one of Ricky's friends said from the back of the class. His friends laughed. But Ricky didn't. He looked like he was concentrating.

When the bell rang at the end of class, everyone jumped up to leave. They were all eager to start working on solving the mystery.

Hannah, Ben, and Corey walked out together. "So what's our first move?" Hannah asked.

"Well, it seems really obvious to me who burned the mascot," Corey said.

"Who?" Ben asked.

"The rival team," he answered. "The Vikings. From Jefferson High School. I mean, that note practically said so."

"You could read that note from across the room?" Hannah asked.

"I have excellent eyesight," Corey said. "Plus, the writing was pretty big."

They headed down the hall toward the cafeteria. "I don't know," Ben said. "It seems a little early in the investigation for suspects. We need more facts."

"Such as?" Corey prompted.

"How did the mascot costume end up on the bonfire?" Ben asked. "Where is it usually kept?"

Corey was about to answer Ben when Hannah said, "Wait. I forgot something." They stopped walking. Ricky Collins passed by.

"What did you forget?" Ben asked as Ricky continued down the hall.

"Nothing," Hannah whispered. "But I noticed Ricky was walking right behind us, eavesdropping. He probably wants to hear what we're going to do, and then he'll try to do it first."

"Maybe we should let him overhear us saying we're going to jump in Green Lake and then dive down to the bottom," Corey suggested. "It's pretty cold this time of year."

Ben and Hannah laughed. Then Corey lowered his voice.

"I was just thinking," he said. "I know the girl who wears the mascot costume for our school."

"Bobby the Bobcat?" Hannah asked.

"Exactly," Corey said. "Her name's Stacey. Maybe she'll know something about where they keep mascot costumes when they're not using them."

"Good idea," Ben said. "Just don't tell Ricky you thought of it."

"He'll be too busy diving to the bottom of Green Lake," Corey said, laughing.

Chapter 4

The three members of Club CSI decided to look for Stacey at lunch.

"That way," Corey explained, "we know she'll be in a good mood."

"Not everyone loves lunch as much as you do," Hannah pointed out.

"Really?" Corey asked, surprised. "That's weird. What's not to love?"

That was a good question. Woodlands Junior High had its own cafeteria run by Mrs. Collins, Ricky's mom. She was an excellent cook, so the food served at lunchtime always tasted good. It was pretty much Corey's favorite part of the school day. Except for maybe forensic science. And gym.

The three friends filled their trays with food.

Corey scanned the tables for Stacey.

"There she is," he said. "Follow me."

But when they reached Stacey's table, all the seats were taken by other girls. They looked up at Corey, wondering what he wanted.

"Hi, Stacey," Corey said in his friendliest voice.

"Hi, Corey," Stacey replied. "What's up?"

Corey felt kind of stupid standing there with his tray full of food. Behind him, Ben and Hannah felt even stupider.

"Well," Corey said, "I was just wondering—"

"Corey," Ben interrupted.

Corey looked around to see what Ben wanted. He saw Ricky approaching with a tray. He was looking around, pretending to be searching for a place to sit down. But there were lots of empty seats nearby. Ricky was eavesdropping again. And Charlie was right behind him.

Corey turned back to Stacey. He lowered his voice. "Could you meet us by the old trophy cases at the end of lunch? It's important."

Stacey looked puzzled. "Okay. I guess so."

Hannah leaned in. "And if Ricky Collins asks you what we talked about, just tell him I wanted to

compliment your sweater. Which is really nice, by the way."

"Thank you," Stacey said, looking even more confused.

Corey raised his voice and spoke a little unnaturally. "Okay, Hannah, you've told her that her sweater is nice. Let's eat our lunch now. I'm sure it will be delicious. Mrs. Collins is such a good cook."

He walked away briskly. Hannah smiled at Stacey and shrugged. Then she and Ben followed Corey to an empty table.

A couple minutes later, Ricky and Charlie sat at a table close to them.

As they ate, the members of Club CSI talked about football, ballet, black holes—anything but the case.

They ate quickly, so they could get to the hallway with the old trophy cases in plenty of time to meet Stacey. Then they got up, carrying their empty trays to the rack. Ricky stood up too.

Before Ricky could catch up with them, Ben whispered to Corey and Hannah, "We'll go separately. See you there." They nodded.

When the three friends left the cafeteria, they

went in three different directions. Ricky watched them go, frustrated.

Hannah sat on the floor, leaning up against one of the wooden cases. The old sports trophies were stored near the end of a hallway that didn't get much use anymore. The doors leading outside were locked.

"How well do you know Stacey?" Hannah asked Corey.

He cocked his head to the side and shrugged. "Not that well."

"Do you think she'll come?" Ben asked.

"Yeah," Corey said.

"How do you know?" Hannah asked. "You said you don't know her that well."

"Everyone loves a mystery," Corey said. "Especially girls."

Hannah tried to decide whether to argue with this. She didn't like it when anyone made generalizations about what girls are supposed to like. But on the other hand, she *did* love mysteries.

Stacey jogged up. "Hi," she said a little

breathlessly. "What's all this about?"

Corey explained that they were trying to win a contest in their forensic class by solving the mystery of who destroyed Rocky the Ram.

"Oh yeah," Stacey said. "I heard about Rocky. Horrible."

"Since you're a mascot too," Corey said, "we thought maybe you could answer a couple of our questions about what you do with your costume."

"Okay," Stacey said. "Like what?"

"Like what do you do with Bobby the Bobcat when you're not at a game or a rally?" Ben asked. "Do you take the outfit to your house?"

Stacey laughed. "No, the costume's too big and heavy to carry around. And I don't think my parents would appreciate having it in their house. Plus, my brothers might mess around with it. Anyway, I change in and out of the costume in the locker room at the gym. The costume stays in its own locker there."

"Do you think that's what they do at the high school, too?" Hannah asked.

Stacey shrugged. "I don't know. Probably. It seems like the easiest thing to do. Those costumes are awkward. And heavy. And hot."

She noticed their puzzled faces. "So you're thinking, 'Then why do you do it?'"

They nodded. That was exactly what they were thinking.

Stacey grinned. "It's still fun. And exciting. You get to be part of every game. And you're part of a school tradition. Plus, it's a tradition in my family too. My older sister was Bobby the Bobcat."

The bell rang. "Gotta go!" Stacey said. "Go, Bobcats!" She ran down the hall, full of energy, jumping and skipping.

"No wonder she's the mascot," Hannah said, watching her go.

Ben thought for a moment. "Since the costumes are kept in gym lockers, maybe after school we should go over to the high school gym."

"Should we meet up separately?" Corey said.

Hannah smiled. "Not a bad idea."

At the end of the school day, Corey closed his locker and then spun the dial on the lock. As he headed outside, he looked around to see if Ricky or Charlie was following him. He was a little disappointed when he didn't see them anywhere. He'd been looking forward to losing them. In fact, he'd spent a fair amount of his time in class that afternoon thinking about how he'd do it—ducking down alleys, hopping over fences, maybe even getting on a city bus and jumping off a block or two later.

He quickly made his way to Woodlands High School. It wasn't far—just a few blocks. It looked different during the day than it had at the rally Friday night. The building seemed bigger than he'd ever noticed before. A little intimidating.

Corey found his way to the gym entrance. He didn't have to wait long until first Hannah and then Ben joined him there.

"Any sign of Ricky?" Corey asked. "Or Charlie?"

"No," Hannah said. "Maybe Ricky lost interest in the investigation already."

"I don't know," Corey said doubtfully. "He seemed pretty psyched about the VIP tickets to the football games."

"Speaking of football," Ben said, "let's find the coach."

They went in. Corey immediately smelled the

familiar smell of a gym: a mix of sweat and the wax they put on the basketball floor to make it shine. There was also a little whiff of chlorine from the pool. He could hear the squeaks of gym shoes on the basketball floor. As an athlete, he felt at home and relaxed. Ben and Hannah felt more nervous.

Inside, a student at a desk looked up from his textbook long enough to have them sign in. He pointed the way to the coach's office and then went back to studying.

Ben knocked on the door. "Come in!" bellowed a gruff voice. They opened the door and went in.

The football coach, a thick-shouldered man with red hair, looked up from his desk. "Yes?" he asked in a hoarse voice that sounded as though he had yelled at a lot of players and referees.

"Excuse us, coach," Corey said. "We wondered if you could answer a couple of questions."

"If you're looking to try out for the football team, you're too late," he said in a growl. "The season's started." Then he looked at them more closely. "Or maybe you're way too early, since it looks like you're not even in high school yet."

Corey wanted to make a good impression on the

coach, since he planned on trying out for this team in a couple of years. "No, sir, we just wanted to ask a couple of questions about the mascot costume. We're investigating its destruction for our forensic class."

"Oh," the coach said. "Whoever did that to Rocky should be punished. That was a terrible act of vandalism. But listen, I'm busy right now. Talk to one of my assistants. They're in the next office."

He went back to studying the papers on his desk. They looked as though they had football plays printed on them. Corey was dying to discuss plays with the coach, but just said "thanks" and backed out of the office.

One of the assistants was happy to answer Club CSI's questions. He even showed them the small side room where the costume was stored between games and rallies. "The costume's a little big for a locker," he explained, "so we keep it in here."

"Is the door usually locked?" Hannah asked.

The assistant shook his head sadly. "No, at least it wasn't before this happened. Now that's going to have to change. It's too bad. People are in and out of this room all the time getting equipment—balls, nets, all kinds of stuff. We never thought anyone would do anything to Rocky. Everybody loves Rocky."

"Almost everybody," Ben pointed out. "Who had access to this room?"

"Pretty much everyone who uses the gym," the assistant answered. "And the gym's open for more hours than the rest of the building, since teams practice here from early in the morning to late at night."

The three investigators looked discouraged. Then Hannah thought of something. "But we had to sign in when we entered the gym. That's a little bit of security."

"Yeah, but it's pretty minimal," the assistant coach admitted. "If you wanted to come in here and vandalize something, it'd be pretty easy to sign someone else's name."

"That's true," Ben agreed.

"So in other words," Corey said, "anyone could have burned Rocky."

"Not me," said the assistant. "I love that ram."

Chapter 5

Miss Hodges scraped a wooden match along the side of a matchbox. The tip of the match burst into flame. The teacher held up the match for the class to see.

"This," she said, "is what we're going to study today. Fire."

She blew the match out, ran it under a faucet, and threw it away. "Why might a crime scene investigator need to know about fire?" she asked.

Ricky raised his hand. "To help him figure out who burned Rocky the Ram," he said.

"So he can score some VIP football tickets," added one of his pals, getting a laugh from his friends. "And share them with his best buddies." Another laugh.

Miss Hodges smiled. "Yes, Ricky, that is one very specific reason why an investigator might need some knowledge of how fire works. Why else?"

Kayla raised her hand. "A criminal might burn down a building or something."

"Good," Miss Hodges said. "And what do we call it when a criminal burns something intentionally?"

"Arson?" Hannah guessed.

"Correct!" Miss Hodges said. She wrote the word on the dry-erase board. "In a suspected case of arson, forensic experts look for the answers to several questions. Did the fire start accidentally, or did someone set it on purpose? Where did the fire start? How did it start? And, of course, if it wasn't an accident, who started it?"

Looking slightly puzzled, Corey raised his hand.

"Yes, Corey?" the teacher said.

"In this case, we already know the answers to those questions," he said. "The firefighters started the bonfire on purpose at the high school with matches. I was there. I saw them do it."

Other students murmured their agreement.

Miss Hodges nodded. "Yes, that's true in this particular case. But today we're talking *generally* about

investigating crime scenes that have involved a fire. We're not just talking about Rocky the Ram."

She picked up her dry-erase marker again. "Let's start with the basics. What do you need for a fire?"

Ryan, one of Ricky's friends in the back of the class, spoke up. "Matches, wood, and maybe some lighter fluid."

"Well, you've got the number right," she said, tossing the marker in the air and then catching it. "You need three things. When it comes to fire, what is wood? Or coal? Or paper?"

"Fuel," Ben said.

"Yes!" Miss Hodges said, writing it on the board. "Fuel! And when you touch a match to fuel, what is the match providing?"

"A flame?" Jennifer volunteered. She didn't sound sure of her answer.

"What's in that flame?" the teacher prodded. "Not cold, but . . ."

"Heat!" Jennifer cried with certainty.

"Exactly!" Miss Hodges said, writing "heat" on the board under "fuel." "That's two. And so there's one more thing you need. What is it?"

Ben was about to speak, but Charlie beat him to

it. "Oxygen," he said. "Fire can't burn in a vacuum."

Everyone was amazed. Not that he got the answer right. Everyone knew he was smart. But that he'd answered the question out loud. Charlie never spoke unless he was called on. Was being partners with Ricky making him less shy?

"That's my partner!" Ricky said, grinning proudly.

"Very good, Charlie," Miss Hodges said as she wrote "oxygen" on the board. "So for a fire you need fuel, heat, and oxygen."

She went on to explain some of the heat sources (matches, candles, cigarettes) and fuels (wood, paper, rags) an arsonist might use. These were items to search for at a burned crime scene.

She also told the class about accelerants—things that make a fire burn faster, like gasoline and kerosene. Sophisticated lab tests could detect traces of accelerants left at the scene of an arson.

"Now let's return to one of those questions I asked at the beginning of class," she said. "Where did the fire start? How might a CSI go about answering that question?"

"I'd search the burned building," Ricky said.

"Looking for what?" Miss Hodges asked.

"The kinds of things you've been talking about," he explained. "An empty gasoline can. A cigarette butt. A lighter."

The three friends in Club CSI were impressed. That was a pretty good answer. Maybe hanging out with Charlie was rubbing off on Ricky.

"Good," Miss Hodges said. "First you'd look for any obvious objects the arsonist might have used to start the fire. But some arsonists are clever. They don't leave clues like that for you to find."

She explained that fire can leave burn trails on floors for the investigator to follow. Fire can flake wood, with smaller particles toward the hottest part of the fire. That can be a clue about where the fire started.

Then Miss Hodges drew a *V* on the board. Since fire rises and spreads, she explained, it can burn a big V on a wall. "The bottom of the *V* points right to where the fire started," she said.

"Now," she continued, turning away from the board, "let's imagine someone's committed arson here in the lab. I've placed a few clues around the room. Please break into your teams and then see what you can find."

There was a chaotic rush as the students found their teammates and started searching the room.

"A match!" Jennifer squealed. "I found a burned match here on the floor!" Miss Hodges reminded her to carefully note where she'd found the match and to pick it up with tweezers and collect it in a plastic bag.

By looking in the trash, Corey found an empty lighter fluid container. Ricky and Charlie found a small, dark *V* on the wall, hidden in a corner. The class agreed that the "fire" (if there had really been one) must have been started there with the match and the lighter fluid.

"Very good!" Miss Hodges said, gesturing for the students to return to their seats. "You're turning into real investigators!"

Kayla raised her hand. "Miss Hodges, I have a question."

"Yes, Kayla?" the teacher said.

"Why?" Kayla asked.

Miss Hodges looked puzzled. "You mean why are you becoming good investigators? You're learning more every day."

"No," Kayla said, shaking her head. "I mean why

would anyone commit arson? What does the criminal get out of it? Whatever someone burns is ruined, so it's not worth anything."

The teacher smiled. "That's an excellent question, Kayla. What do you think, class?"

"Some weirdos just really love fire," Ryan said. "They're, like, obsessed with it."

"That's true," Miss Hodges said. She wrote "pyro-mania" on the board. "Some experts think it might give them a feeling of power to start a fire. Why else might an arsonist start a fire?"

"Revenge?" Ricky said. "To get back at someone?"

"Yes," Miss Hodges said, writing "revenge" on the board.

"Insurance fraud," Corey suggested. He'd heard an uncle of his talking about a criminal burning down a building to get the insurance money.

"Very good," Miss Hodges said, writing "fraud" on the board. "Now I'm going to write down another word. Can anyone tell me what it means?"

The class watched as she wrote "spoliation."

Everyone was stumped. Even Ben and Charlie.

"Aha!" Miss Hodges said. "I've stumped you!"

"Spoliation," Ryan said from the back of the

room, "is when you spoliate something. My sister exspoliates her face every night."

"I think you mean 'exfoliates,'" Hannah said. "That's when you scrub away the dead skin cells."

"It doesn't help her face any," Ryan said, getting a laugh from his friends.

Miss Hodges rapped her knuckles next to the word "spoliation" on the board. She said, "'Spoliation,' as the term is used by forensic scientists, means the destruction of evidence. And sometimes spoliation is a reason for arson."

"So the criminal starts a fire to burn up the evidence of some other crime he's committed?" Hannah clarified.

"That's exactly right," Miss Hodges confirmed.

Ben raised his hand.

"Yes, Ben?"

"Is anyone thinking that's what happened in the case of Rocky the Ram?" he asked.

Miss Hodges cocked her head, thinking. "I doubt it," she said. "This wasn't a case of arson. The fire was set carefully and safely by professionals. The only crimes here seem to be the theft and the destruction of the costume."

"Maybe whoever stole the costume burned it to

cover up the theft," Corey said, thinking out loud.

"That doesn't make any sense," Ricky protested. He pretended to be the thief and said, "Oh no! I've accidentally stolen Rocky the Ram! I'd better burn him up!" Several kids laughed.

"I was just tossing out an idea," Corey grumbled.

"Yeah, I think that's the right thing to do with that idea," Ricky said. "Toss it out."

"We're just about out of time," Miss Hodges said. "Tonight I'd like you to read the section on fire forensics in your textbook. See if it gives you any ideas about the mascot case. I'd also recommend that you do a little research to see if any similar crimes have been committed in the past here in town. That's one of the things a real CSI team would do at this stage."

The bell rang, and the students headed out of the lab. As they went, one of Ricky's pals joked, "Maybe there's a serial mascot-costume burner on the loose in Nevada!"

His friends laughed, but Ricky didn't. Ben suspected he and Charlie were going to do the research suggested by Miss Hodges.

Well, they wouldn't be the only ones. . . .

Chapter 6

After school, Ben, Hannah, and Corey headed to the public library. It was a windy, cool afternoon, so they were happy to go through the front doors into the warm, brightly lit building.

The library was one of the older buildings in town, with big pillars out front and lots of wood inside. Some people thought the town should build a new, modern library, but Hannah liked the old one. She'd been coming here since her parents brought her to the children's section when she was little. The day she'd gotten her own library card, she'd felt so proud and excited.

"What are we looking for?" Corey whispered.

"Local crimes against school mascots," Ben whispered back. "We're trying to find out if anything like the destruction of Rocky the Ram has happened around here before."

"I'll start on the Internet," Hannah said, heading for one of the library's computers.

Corey looked puzzled. "Couldn't we have just used the Internet at home?" he asked.

Ben nodded. "Sure, but not everything's on the Internet. The library's got files of information on this town that date way back. Come on, I'll show you."

Ben showed Corey the library's collections of clippings and newspaper articles. "Why can't they just scan all this stuff and put it on the Internet?" Corey asked.

A librarian, who was shelving books nearby, overheard them. "We don't have the time. Or money," she said. "What are you looking for?" With her help, Ben and Corey started searching for any stories related to the town's sports mascots over the years.

It took a while. But after almost an hour of hunting . . .

"Aha!" Corey said loudly. He instantly remembered he was in the library and then looked around only to see the librarian glaring at him. He silently mouthed the words *I'm sorry*.

Hannah and Ben had heard his outburst, so they quickly joined him to see what he'd found. In front of him was a big folder labeled "Weird Crimes." It was one of many folders covering the town's history.

In his hand he was holding a piece of thin cardboard. It had an old newspaper article glued to it. The paper had turned brown, but you could still read the headline: "Mascot Costume Burned."

"It's from twenty-five years ago!" Corey whispered excitedly.

"What happened?" Hannah asked.

"Believe it or not, almost exactly the same thing," Corey said. "Somebody stole the Rocky the Ram costume and then burned it on a pep rally bonfire the night before the game against Jefferson High School!"

"No way!" Ben said. He could scarcely believe an identical crime had been committed twenty-five years earlier, but there it was, right in the newspaper.

"Did they ever find out who did it?" Hannah asked.

"Let's see," Corey said, looking through the folder. "Here it is!"

He held up another piece of cardboard. The article glued to it had a headline that read "Mascot Case Solved."

The three friends practically clunked their heads together moving in to read the article. It said that "players from the rival Jefferson High School football squad confessed to the act of vandalism. The Vikings agreed to replace the costume."

Corey looked up from the article, nodding and smiling. "See?" he said. "I told you the Vikings did it."

"Just because they did it back then doesn't mean they did it this time," Ben pointed out. He was always very careful about jumping to conclusions before they'd gathered all the evidence.

"Still, it *is* a pretty amazing coincidence," Hannah said.

"Maybe it's not a coincidence at all," Ben suggested. "Maybe whoever burned the costume this time knew about the incident twenty-five years ago."

"You mean a copycat crime?" Hannah asked.

"It could be," Ben said. "But we definitely need more evidence."

Corey held up the two articles. "I think this is an amazing piece of evidence. I mean, if the Vikings didn't burn Rocky the Ram, who did?"

"How about that guy?" Hannah said. Corey and Ben looked to see who she was talking about. It was Logan Canfield, the kid from the pep rally who'd complained so intensely about Mitchell. He was sitting at a table studying by himself.

"Logan?" Corey asked doubtfully. "Why would Logan burn the costume? He loves Rocky the Ram!"

"Maybe he wanted to make Mitchell look bad," Hannah said. "He figured Mitchell would get blamed, so when the school bought a new costume, they wouldn't let Mitchell wear it. And then Logan could step in and take over as Rocky."

"I don't know . . . ," Corey said.

"I say it's worth talking to him," Ben said. "Come on."

Ben grabbed his backpack and headed toward the table Logan was sitting at. Corey and Hannah quickly gathered up their stuff and then followed him.

"Hey, Logan," Ben greeted. "How's it going?"

Logan looked up, startled to see three junior

high kids standing over him. "Who are you?" he asked.

"We met at the pep rally last Friday night, remember?" Hannah asked, smiling sweetly.

"You were talking about how Mitchell shouldn't be Rocky the Ram," Corey added.

"Oh yeah," Logan said. Here in the library, he didn't seem nearly as enthusiastic about criticizing Mitchell.

"Did you hear about what happened to the costume?" Corey asked.

"Yeah," Logan said, looking away.

"Excuse me," said the librarian, who had walked right up without them noticing. "If the four of you want to talk, I'm afraid you'll have to leave the library."

"Sorry," Hannah whispered. She turned back to Logan. "Do you want to go outside and talk?"

"What about?" he asked.

"Rocky the Ram," she said.

Logan frowned. He thought about it for a second, then nodded. He started to gather up his books and put them into his backpack. He stood up, put on his jacket, and gestured for Club CSI to lead the way.

Outside, it was still windy and even chillier. They found a corner of the building that seemed to be out of the wind. Mostly. Until it changed direction.

"So, what do you think happened, exactly?" Ben asked casually.

Logan looked slightly annoyed. "I *know* what happened. Somebody threw the costume on the bonfire so it'd burned up."

"You didn't see it happen, did you?" Corey inquired.

Logan looked at Corey like he was crazy. "Of course not. Otherwise I would've reported it. Or stopped them." He shook his head. "This never would have happened if they hadn't picked Mitchell to be the mascot."

"Why do you say that?" Hannah asked.

"Isn't it obvious?" Logan said. "Mitchell didn't put on the costume that night, so someone was able to steal it and then burn it. It's all his fault. He should have taken better care of Rocky. I would have, if they'd picked me."

He picked up a pebble and then tossed it at a tree. He missed.

"Did you ever hear about the other time this happened?" Ben asked. "Twenty-five years ago?"

Logan nodded. "Sure. Anyone who's studied the history of Rocky the Ram knows about that. Of course, I doubt Mitchell knows about it. Listen, I've gotta go."

Without another word, he walked away. The members of Club CSI waited until he was out of earshot before they said anything.

"Nice guy," Corey remarked, not meaning it.

"Friendly," Hannah added.

"Everything he said fits with Hannah's theory about him wanting to make Mitchell look bad," Ben observed. "Pretty much all he wanted to talk about was what a bad mascot Mitchell was."

"Yeah," Corey said. "And he knew about the burning twenty-five years ago."

"I say he's still a suspect," Hannah concluded.

The two guys agreed with her. But they needed evidence. And Corey still thought the players at Jefferson High School were the best suspects.

"Remember the player we spotted at the rally?" he said. "The one hanging around that tree, spying?"

"What makes you think he was spying?" Ben asked.

"He looked suspicious," Corey said.

"Maybe," said Hannah. "But I didn't see him carrying a ram costume."

They started walking home.

"No," Corey said. "But maybe later, after we saw him, he sneaked into the gym, stole the costume, and slipped it into the bonfire before the firefighters put it out. Then he pinned that note to the tree."

"I guess it's possible," Ben said. "But before we tackle a bunch of football players—"

"So to speak," Hannah interrupted.

Ben looked puzzled.

"Tackle?" Hannah said. "Football players?"

Ben got it. "Oh right. Anyway, before we . . . question them, I think we need more evidence."

"More evidence, more evidence," Corey echoed. "You *always* think we need more evidence."

"You can never have too much evidence," Ben said. "And tomorrow in class, Miss Hodges is going to let us examine the burned costume and the note."

"Cool," Corey said, kicking at leaves on the sidewalk. "And since I didn't see any of our classmates at the library, I'll bet we'll be the only ones who'll know about the burning twenty-five years ago!"

Chapter 7

They weren't.

As soon as they arrived at forensic science class the next day, they heard Ricky talking about how the mascot had been burned twenty-five years earlier.

"How did he find out?" Hannah asked Ben and Corey. "He definitely wasn't at the library when we were there. I would've heard him. Listen to that loud voice."

Ricky was telling a couple of kids that the earlier crime was exactly like the one they were investigating.

"Maybe he got there after we left," Corey offered.

"Dude," Ryan was saying to Ricky. "How'd you find out about this stuff?"

Ricky smiled proudly. "My dad. He knew all about it. At dinner I remembered we were supposed to research whether there'd been any similar crimes, so I brought it up. And he told me about the time twenty-five years ago when the costume got burned. He was in school then, so he remembered the whole thing."

"That's your research?" Ryan asked. "Asking your dad at dinner?"

"What research did *you* do?" Ricky accused.

Ryan shrugged. It was obvious he hadn't done any research at all.

"We only talked about it at the end of dinner, and then he had to go to work," Ricky said. His dad worked a night shift at a bakery. "I'll bet he knows tons more about it. Our team is *definitely* going to win. Right, partner?"

Ricky punched Charlie's arm. Charlie managed to smile and nod before he walked away, rubbing his arm.

Other kids in the class surrounded Ricky, pumping him for information about the incident that had occurred twenty-five years before. Apparently, none of them had come up with any similar crimes in their research.

Ricky spotted Club CSI standing together, watching him. "Hey, Club See Us Lose!" he called across the room. "Don't you want to hear about my killer research?"

"No, thanks," Hannah replied. "We did our own."

As they sat down, Corey said, "Well, at least it sounds as though he didn't learn anything we didn't already know."

"Yeah," Ben said, "but I've got a feeling Ricky and Charlie might provide some tough competition."

"But a little competition is good, remember?" Corey reminded them.

Miss Hodges brought the class to order. "Hello, class. I hope you all read the section in our textbook about fire forensics. It may prove useful today."

Jennifer asked, "We're going to examine the mascot costume, right?"

Miss Hodges smiled, nodding. "Yes, the costume and the note. First we'll examine them together as a group, and then each team will have some time alone with the evidence to do their own examinations."

She walked across the room to open the door to her small office. "Okay," she said. "We're ready." She turned back to the class and said, "I've got a special assistant today: Principal Inverno."

The principal came out of Miss Hodges's office, carrying the garbage bag. "Good morning!" he said cheerfully.

"I needed someone to supervise your individual sessions with the evidence, so Principal Inverno very kindly agreed to help," Miss Hodges explained.

"Happy to do it," Principal Inverno said. "After all, I'm the one who brought you this smelly mess in the first place."

Without thinking, some of the students sat up straighter in their seats. They weren't used to having the principal of the school in their classroom.

"All right," Miss Hodges said as she pulled the burned costume out of the black garbage bag. "Let's begin our examination of Rocky the Ram."

She laid the costume out on a table. "Gather around," she said, inviting them up for a closer look.

The students got up and gathered around the table. At first the costume just looked like a blackened mess. But as they stared at it, they started to make out some of its features—the hooves, the fur, and the horns on the oversize head.

"Maybe one of us should put it on," Ryan said, daring to make a joke with the principal right there.

"Are you volunteering?" Principal Inverno asked. The students laughed.

"Normally I don't allow you to use your phones during class," Miss Hodges said. "But I encourage you to take pictures, just as real CSI investigators would."

The students whipped out their phones and started to click away. They jostled for good positions, trying to snap photos from the best angles.

"Please don't touch the evidence," Miss Hodges said. "You'll be able to during your team's individual examination, but for now, just use your eyes. You might want to take notes."

Several students got out their notebooks and started writing.

"Anyone notice anything they'd like to share with the class?" Miss Hodges asked.

But since they were all competing with one another, everyone kept their thoughts to themselves. No one wanted to give anything good away to the other teams.

"It's definitely been burned," Ricky said.

A couple of kids laughed, but Miss Hodges said, "Actually, that's an important observation. Just because it was found at the site of a bonfire doesn't prove that it was thrown on the bonfire while it was still burning."

"I smell that it'd been burned," Ryan said. "I don't need to see it."

"But it might smell burned just from being in the ashes," Charlie pointed out. "That doesn't prove it'd been burned."

Charlie standing up to Ryan? He was getting bolder every day.

"Very good, Charlie," Miss Hodges said. "We can't always trust just one of our senses. We need confirmation from as many senses as possible. Smell, sight, touch . . ."

"Taste?" Charlie said, smiling. Now Charlie was making jokes. The world had turned upside down.

Miss Hodges smiled back. "Only if we have a volunteer." The class laughed.

"All right," she said. "I think that's long enough for our group examination. Principal Inverno?"

The principal put the costume back into the bag and then carried it into the little office. Meanwhile,

Miss Hodges laid out some ground rules.

"Each team will have a brief period of time alone with the costume and the note, supervised by Principal Inverno. You may touch the costume. You may even take small samples, but it's important that you leave enough for the other teams. If, for example, there's a section of fur with a stain on it, you may collect a few hairs, but leave plenty for the others. Club CSI, you're up first."

Ricky looked disappointed to not be first. "Remember, leave plenty of evidence for us!" he called out.

"You got it," Corey said as he followed Hannah and Ben into the office. They closed the door behind them.

Inside, Principal Inverno had laid the costume on Miss Hodges's desk. Ben noticed immediately that the desk had been cleared off and covered with a plastic tarp. "Ah, Club CSI," the principal said. "Rocky's all yours." He stood in the corner of the office with his arms folded across his chest.

At first it felt a little weird being crammed into the small office with the principal and the smoky-smelling costume. But once they started concentrating on their examination, Club CSI almost forgot the principal was there.

Hannah began by taking more pictures with her cell phone. She thoroughly covered the costume, recording every inch. Halfway through, Ben and Corey turned the costume over so she could get the other side.

"Let's check the inside, too," Ben said. They couldn't turn the costume inside out, but they did manage to peer inside it. They didn't find anything unusual.

"I don't see any stains on the fur," Corey said. "Just scorch and burn marks."

"We'll gather a few hairs from different parts of the costume," Hannah said. They put the hairs in plastic bags to examine later.

"The head doesn't seem as badly burned," Corey noticed. All three of them examined the head more closely. It looked squished down. The frame inside the head was flattened.

"What's this?" Ben said, leaning over the head to peer at it closely. Hannah and Corey looked too.

"Looks like little pieces of glass," Hannah observed.

"And pebbles," Corey added.

"There's also dirt and possibly some oil," Ben said. "Let's get some close-ups and some samples."

Hannah took close-up photos of the ram's head. Ben carefully plucked out a few samples of the materials they'd found stuck in the head and then put them in plastic bags.

The note that the custodians had found pinned to the tree was lying on a small side table. Club CSI studied it carefully and took pictures.

"It's definitely handwritten," Hannah remarked. "But the handwriting is very neat and clear."

"Looks as though whoever wrote it used an ordinary marker," Corey said. "There's nothing weird looking about the ink."

Principal Inverno looked at his watch. "Okay, time's up," he said. "Let's get the next team in here."

Chapter 8

Before the last period of the day, Hannah, Ben, and Corey met by the old trophy lockers to discuss what they'd seen in their examination of the mascot costume.

"I think the most interesting thing we found was the stuff on the head," Hannah said. "The little pieces of rock and glass and mud. I don't see how those kinds of things could come out of a bonfire."

Sitting on the floor, Corey bounced a tennis ball against the wall and then caught it. He carried a ball in his backpack for moments like these. His coach said it was good for hand-eye coordination.

He just thought it was fun.

"I agree," he said. "A fire wouldn't put junk like

that on the costume. Although maybe the janitors who found it dragged it across the parking lot or something."

"I did some research online during my free period," Ben said. "The materials we found on the costume are just the sorts of things you'd commonly find in the treads of a car's tires."

"Car tires?" Hannah asked. "Hold on a second." She pulled her phone out of her backpack. She flipped through her pictures of the costume. She stopped when she got to one, and used her thumb and forefinger to expand the picture, zooming in on the area that interested her.

"There," she said. "I thought these marks on the head looked kind of familiar. What would you say they are?"

Corey and Ben leaned in to look at her phone. "A tire track!" Ben said. "Good eye, Hannah."

"A tire track?" Corey repeated. "You mean, before the costume was tossed on the bonfire, it was run over by a car?"

"Sure looks like it," Hannah said.

"Wow," Corey said. "Someone really wanted to ruin Rocky."

The more they stared at the picture on Hannah's phone, the more certain they became that they were looking at a tire track.

"Being run over by a car would definitely explain why Rocky's head looked squished," Hannah noted.

"I say it's time to talk to the football players over at Jefferson," Corey said, tossing his ball with his right hand and catching it with his left.

"Why them?" Hannah asked.

"Well," he said, "they've always been my number one suspects. But now that we see this, it makes even more sense. They're old enough to have driver's licenses. And cars. They could have driven over Rocky, thrown him into the trunk, taken him to the rally, and when no one was looking, tossed him into the bonfire before the firefighters doused it."

"True," Ben said. "But so could just about any high school student over the age of sixteen. Or any adult, for that matter."

"You know who I think we should talk to?" Hannah asked.

"Who?" Corey wondered.

"The kid who was supposed to wear the costume at the rally."

"Mitchell? Why him?"

"It just makes sense," Hannah explained. "He knows more about that ram costume than anybody. He should be the first person we talk to. Why wasn't he at the rally? Where was he?"

Corey nodded. Talking to Mitchell did seem like a logical move.

"Okay, so it's settled," Ben said. "After school, we'll go back to the high school to talk to Mitchell."

"Okay," Corey said, "but I won't recognize him without his ram costume on."

As it turned out, it wasn't that hard to track down Mitchell. Lots of people at the high school knew which guy was Rocky the Ram.

Getting him to talk was a little harder.

"Look, I already talked to some kids from your class," Mitchell complained. He was a short guy with curly brown hair and ears that stuck out from the sides of his head.

"You did?" Corey said. "Who?"

"I forget their names," Mitchell said. "A big guy and a smaller guy with glasses."

"Ricky and Charlie?" Hannah asked, exchanging quick looks with Ben and Corey.

Mitchell nodded. "Yeah, that sounds right. And like I told them, I have no idea how the costume ended up on the bonfire. I wasn't even there."

He started to walk away, but Club CSI walked with him.

"Why weren't you there?" Hannah asked. "I mean, they really missed you. Everybody was asking where the mascot was. They all love the way you do Rocky the Ram." She figured a little flattery wouldn't hurt.

Mitchell took the bait. "Really?" he asked. "They like how I do it?"

"They say you're the best Rocky ever," Hannah continued, her fingers crossed behind her back.

"Well," he said, "I wasn't there because there was no point. The costume was missing."

"When was the last time you saw the costume?" Ben asked.

Mitchell paused and leaned up against a tree, thinking. "The weekend before. I wore it for the away game against Farrow High. When we got back, I put it in the storage room."

"Did you see it during the week between the

Farrow game and the pep rally?" Corey asked.

Mitchell shook his head. "The next time I went in the storage room to get it was the day of the pep rally. It was gone. I told one of the assistant coaches, and then I went home."

"Why didn't you stay for the rally?" Hannah asked.

He shrugged. "I don't know. I guess I was embarrassed. I knew everyone would be asking me why I wasn't dressed as Rocky the Ram, and I didn't even know where the costume was."

Corey looked puzzled. "But that wasn't your fault. We heard they don't lock the storage room and that tons of people go in and out of the gym every day."

"Yeah, that's true," Mitchell said.

"So who do you think took it?" Corey asked.

Mitchell raised his eyebrows and held his hands out. "Everybody knows who took it! The Vikings! They said so right on that note!"

"Couldn't someone else have written that note?" Ben said.

Mitchell shook his head emphatically. "The Vikings did it, just like they did twenty-five years ago. Have you heard about that?"

The members of Club CSI nodded. "We read about it at the library," Ben said.

"I'm surprised you hadn't already heard about it," Mitchell said. "It was a huge deal back then. It's one of the first things they tell you about when you become the mascot. It's, like, a legend!"

"So you think the Vikings did it again this time, just like they did twenty-five years ago," Hannah summed up.

"Definitely," Mitchell said. "You know, nice costumes like Rocky the Ram cost thousands of dollars. The Vikings who did it will probably end up going to prison."

That seemed pretty unlikely. The three friends had never heard of anyone going to prison for destroying a mascot costume. But Mitchell seemed to believe it, so they didn't argue with him.

"Of course, for thousands of dollars they could make the costume a lot more comfortable," Mitchell complained. "It's heavy, and really hot, and it smells bad. The mascot has to jump around a lot, but they can't just send a costume like that to the cleaner's after every game."

"If it's so awful being the mascot, why do you

do it?" Hannah asked. Mitchell didn't seem like the kind of student who was filled with school spirit.

For the first time, Mitchell smiled a little. "Well," he said, "the mascot gets to hang out with the cheerleaders."

Corey grinned. "Ever score any dates with the cheerleaders?"

"No," Mitchell admitted. "Not yet. And now with the costume destroyed, my chances don't look too good."

He looked at his watch. "It's getting late. I've gotta get home."

"Okay," Ben said. "Thanks for answering our questions."

"No problem," Mitchell said. "Hope you get an A."

Chapter 9

The next morning, Club CSI walked to school together. It was a beautiful fall day in Nevada, with the sun shining.

"The more I think about it," Corey said, "the more I think the football players over at Jefferson wrecked Rocky."

"Just like it said on the note?" Hannah asked.

"Exactly," Corey said. "Sometimes the most obvious answer is the correct answer."

Ben frowned. "It didn't actually say that on the note. It just said 'Vikings Rule.' It didn't say 'We, the Jefferson High School Vikings, destroyed this costume.'"

"Okay," Corey admitted. "But who turned out to be the culprits twenty-five years ago? The Vikings!"

"The Vikings turned out to be the culprits when it came to raiding Europe in the ninth century too, but I doubt they destroyed Rocky the Ram!" Ben said.

Corey stared at Ben. "You know," he said, "if you ever expect to date anyone in high school, you're going to have to stop saying things like that."

Hannah laughed. "Hey, maybe Ben will date history buffs!"

Ben was a little embarrassed, but he smiled.

"All I'm saying is that we go talk to the football players at Jefferson to see if we can figure out whether they did it," Corey insisted.

"Fine," Ben said, relieved to have the subject changed from his future dating prospects. "We'll go after school today."

"And who knows?" Corey added. "Maybe you'll meet some history buffs!"

Miss Hodges held up a blank piece of paper. "What can you tell me about this?"

The students in her forensic science class stared

at her for a moment. What was there to say about a blank piece of paper?

"It's a blank piece of paper?" Jennifer said, sounding more like she was asking a question than answering one.

"Yes," Miss Hodges said. "It is a blank piece of paper. But if a CSI found this piece of paper at a crime scene, he or she would want to determine some of its specific qualities to help identify where the paper might have come from."

She put down the piece of paper and then picked up an unopened package of paper. "For example, the wrapper on this package describes a few of the paper's qualities."

Miss Hodges pointed to a number on the wrapper. "See this eighty-eight?" she asked. The students nodded. "That's the paper's brightness. This paper reflects back about eighty-eight percent of the light you shine on it."

She slid her finger down the package. "There's a smaller number here that you may not be able to see: one hundred and twenty-five. That's the paper's whiteness. Whiteness is the shade of white that the manufacturer has made the paper by bleaching the wood pulp. There are three main shades of whiteness: balanced white, warm white, and blue white."

Many of the students were taking notes. As Miss Hodges described the specific qualities of paper, they couldn't help but take a closer look at the paper in the notebooks they were writing on. They'd never really thought about paper's qualities before. It seemed as though every time you looked at a subject, no matter how small, it turned out there was a whole world of information about it. This time it was the World of Paper.

The teacher pointed to the package of paper again. "And there's another number here: twenty. That's the paper's weight. Five hundred sheets of this paper—or a ream—should weigh twenty pounds."

She looked at the students. "How thick is paper?"

"Not very," Ryan said, getting a laugh from his friends.

"Actually, Ryan, you're right," Miss Hodges said. "The thickness of paper is measured by the thousandth of an inch. This measurement is called the paper's caliper."

She turned to the dry-erase board and wrote "caliper." Then she turned back to the class.

"So paper has brightness, whiteness, weight, and caliper. And that's just to start with! In the laboratory, investigators can use advanced technology to analyze all the chemicals in a piece of paper." She paused a moment. "But why would they do that?"

Ben raised his hand. "If they could match a piece of paper from a crime scene to a pad of paper in a suspect's home, that might help convict the suspect."

Miss Hodges nodded. "Yes, Ben. Very good."

She spread several different pads of paper on the table. Some had white paper and some had yellow. Some had lines and some didn't. A couple had holes punched in the sides.

"Each of these pads of paper has a big letter printed on it. See?" She held up a pad with a large *A* on it. She set the pad back on the table.

Miss Hodges picked up a brown paper bag. She turned it over. Lots of small pieces of papers fluttered out.

"And each of these pieces of paper has a number printed on it," she said. "Let's see how well you can do without any advanced technology. Just use your eyes. Look at the pieces of paper and then write down which pad each piece came from. Match each number to a letter. You can work in your teams if you'd like."

The students hurried to pick up the pieces of paper. They compared them to the pads and started writing down the letters that went with each number.

Some of the pieces of paper had obviously come from one of the pads—they were the same color, with the same lines and punched-out holes. But others were trickier. Corey moved one piece of paper back and forth between two pads, comparing them.

"Definitely *C*," Hannah said to him, quietly.

"Really?" he asked. "I was going to go with *D*."

"I was kind of thinking *E*," Ben admitted.

They went with *C*. Hannah seemed so sure.

And when Miss Hodges gave them the answers, Hannah was right. She had a very good eye for color.

After they'd learned about paper, Miss Hodges told them a bit about ink. She talked about the different kinds of writing instruments—ballpoint pens, roller-ball pens, felt-tip markers—and the different kinds of inks they used.

Then she put her students through another exercise, trying to match marks made with different kinds of pens. A few of the inks looked the same until the students put them under an ultraviolet light. The UV rays helped them see the differences in the inks that they couldn't see under regular light.

"Now," she said, "let's talk about handwriting."

Kayla raised her hand. "Ooh, I've heard that you can tell a person's personality from their handwriting."

"That could be," Miss Hodges said. "But that's not really what the CSI is interested in. He or she is trying to find out who wrote the ransom note or the threatening letter or the grocery list dropped at the scene of the crime. How might a CSI do that?"

Charlie's hand shot up.

"Yes, Charlie?"

"The investigator would compare handwriting from the suspects to the handwriting found at the crime scene," he answered.

"That's right. Excellent," Miss Hodges said. "Investigators compare a suspect's handwriting

sample—called 'a standard'—to the unidentified handwriting, hoping for a match."

She turned back to the dry-erase board and wrote "standard."

"There are two types of handwriting standards," she continued, "requested and nonrequested. Which do you think is preferred?"

The class thought about this. Slowly, Hannah raised her hand.

"Yes, Hannah?"

"Nonrequested."

"Why?"

"Because if you ask someone to give you a handwriting sample, they might try to change their handwriting so it doesn't match," Hannah said. "But if you could get a nonrequested sample, you could be more sure it was in the person's real handwriting."

"Terrific!" Miss Hodges said. "That's exactly right."

She went on to describe how handwriting analysts looked at each letter's shape, size, and slant. She also talked about how to tell if a writer is right- or left-handed.

"Okay," she said. "I want two requested standards from each of you. The first can be anything you want. Just write down a couple of sentences. For the second one, please copy this sentence."

She turned back to the dry-erase board and wrote, "The quick brown fox jumps over the lazy dog."

"Can anyone tell me something interesting about this sentence?"

Corey actually knew the answer, though he didn't remember how he knew. He thought maybe he'd heard his mother mention this sentence. Something about a typing class she took a long time ago. He raised his hand. "It has every letter in the alphabet."

"That's right," Miss Hodges said. "Please just write both samples naturally. Don't think about your handwriting. And definitely don't try to change your handwriting between the two samples. That'll ruin everything. When you're done, please bring them up here. Put the 'quick brown fox'es in this pile, and your original sentences in this pile."

The students wrote quickly and then carried their little slips of paper up to the front table. Miss Hodges shuffled the slips (keeping them in their separate piles) and then had the students try to match the handwriting samples.

Some were easy. Jennifer, for example, had very

nice, clear handwriting, so they could spot her two samples right away.

Others were not only hard to match, they were hard to read.

"Some people in this class have *terrible* handwriting," Kayla complained as she stared at the slips of paper.

"We're not here to judge the quality of the handwriting, just to match the samples," Miss Hodges reminded them.

At the end of the period, everyone agreed it'd been another fun class, kind of like doing puzzles.

But Ben was thinking it was more than just fun. It could be very useful for figuring out who left the note on the tree near the bonfire.

Unfortunately, Charlie was thinking the exact same thing. Ben heard him say to Ricky as they were leaving, "We should get handwriting standards from the chief suspects."

"Great idea, partner!" Ricky said, slapping him on the back.

Not if Club CSI could get them first . . .

Chapter 10

Jefferson High School was on the other side of town, so Hannah, Ben, and Corey went home first to get their bicycles. It wasn't easy talking to one another while they rode, but they managed to shout a few sentences when they were on quiet streets.

"What exactly are we going to say to these football players?" Hannah yelled.

"Yeah," Ben said. "We can't just walk up to them and ask if they destroyed Rocky the Ram."

"I figured we'd play it by ear," Corey replied.

"I think we should have some kind of plan," Hannah said.

They rode on in silence for a block or two.

"Corey, you're the football player," said Ben.

"Right," Corey said. "I remember."

"So, maybe you can use that," Ben suggested.

"Okay," agreed Corey. "Good idea." Then he tried to figure out how he could use being a football player to talk to the high school guys.

The football team was out practicing on their field. Club CSI locked up their bikes and then walked over to the football field. When the players took a break, Corey led the way over to a few of them.

"Hey," he said. "Kind of hot for practice."

"Nah, it's okay," said one of the players. He grabbed a bottle of water and took a long drink.

"I was kind of thinking of going out for football when I get to high school," Corey said. He didn't mention he'd be going to Woodlands, not Jefferson. "Is it a lot harder than junior high football?"

"The guys are a lot bigger," one of them said.

"They tackle harder," another added.

"And the coaches are much, much meaner," said a third. They all laughed.

Corey laughed too. "Hey, great game against Woodlands last Saturday, by the way." It killed Corey to say this, but he wanted to get them talking about last weekend.

"Thanks," one of the players said. "We had a good day."

"And the Rams had a lousy one," another player said. More laughs.

"Maybe they were upset about their mascot being burned," Corey said. "That was pretty crazy. I wonder who the mastermind behind that was."

He was hoping maybe the players would start talking about the destruction of Rocky the Ram. Ben and Hannah could watch them carefully to see if they looked sly or proud. Or if they quickly grinned. Something that would give them away. Maybe they'd even brag about burning the costume.

But they didn't do any of those things.

"That was terrible," one of the players said, shaking his head.

"Horrible," another added.

"Yeah, that was not cool at all," a third said. "Those mascots work really hard. I liked Rocky the Ram."

"That dumb note made people think we did it," another player said. "Which is ridiculous. We're on the team to win football games. Not play stupid pranks on people."

"Yeah, I really hate it that people think we did that," the first player said. He looked at Corey, Ben, and Hannah. "Hey, *you* don't think we did it, do you?"

Corey shook his head. "No way. Of course not."

Hannah said, "I guess maybe people think the rivalry between Jefferson and Woodlands just got out of hand."

A big player said, "To tell the truth, the biggest rivalry was between the mascots. Our Viking and their ram."

Some of the players laughed. "Yeah," one of them said. "Steve really hates Rocky the Ram for some reason."

"Who's Steve?" Hannah asked.

"The guy who wears the Viking costume," another player explained. "At the game against Woodlands last year, he actually got into a fight with Rocky. We had to separate them. Luckily, they couldn't really hurt each other with those big heads on."

All the players laughed.

Ben thought of something. "We saw a lot of cool cars in the parking lot. Do some of you guys have your own cars?"

A few of the guys nodded proudly.

"Does Steve?" Hannah asked.

They weren't sure, but a couple of them thought Steve did have his own car. Or at least access to his family's car.

Hannah looked around and noticed the player they'd seen behind the tree at the pep rally. She managed to get Ben's attention, nodding toward the player.

"Well, let's not bother these guys anymore," Ben said to Corey. "Let's go."

"Thanks, guys," Corey said. "Good talking to you."

"Maybe we'll see you on the team in a couple of years," one of the players said.

"Yeah," Corey said. "Maybe."

"Try to get bigger," the player suggested. Some of his friends chuckled.

Hannah, Ben, and Corey hurried over to where the player from the pep rally was sitting by himself. He saw them coming and ran out onto the field. An assistant coach blew his whistle. Break was over.

But Club CSI was patient. They waited until football practice ended. When they saw the player they wanted to talk to coming out of the gym in his

street clothes, they followed him until they could speak to him alone.

"Excuse me," Hannah said. "My name is Hannah. These are my friends Ben and Corey. Could we ask you something?"

The player looked startled. "Oh, hi. I'm Chris. What do you need to talk to me about?"

"About the pep rally last Friday," Ben said. "At Woodlands."

Chris looked around to see if anyone was listening. No one else was around. "What about it?"

"We saw you," Corey said. "Behind a tree. What were you doing there?"

Chris sighed. It looked as though he were about to confess.

And he was. Just not to burning Rocky the Ram.

"My cousin plays in the marching band at Woodlands," he said quietly. "I really wanted to see her perform. I know I shouldn't have gone to a rally for the rival team, but she's so proud of being in the band, and I wanted to support her."

"Oh," Hannah said. "That's really nice."

Nice, but not incriminating, thought Ben.

Chapter 11

As they rode their bikes away from Jefferson High School, the three friends talked about what they'd just found out.

"No one acted at all guilty," Hannah said, pedaling smoothly to stay near Ben and Corey.

"And Chris had a good reason to be at the rally," Corey added.

"A very nice reason," Hannah said.

"Still, we didn't learn anything that would eliminate the Jefferson football players as suspects," Ben said.

"No," Hannah said, "but I thought the stuff they told us about Steve the angry Viking mascot was really interesting."

"Where are we headed?" Corey asked.

"Let's go to my house," Ben said. "We can use my computer to take a closer look at our pictures of the note."

"Sounds good," Corey said. "Race you!"

He took off pedaling. Hannah and Ben let him go. They already knew he was the fastest. They'd see him at Ben's house, where he'd probably talk Ben's mom into giving him a snack.

Corey's mouth was full with a chocolate-chip cookie. "That could be just about anybody's printing," he said, chewing.

The three of them were staring at the big monitor on Ben's desk. On it was a picture of the note the custodians had found pinned to the tree on the morning after the bonfire.

"See anything unusual?" Ben asked.

"Well, you can't really see this in our photo, but I remember the note was on heavy paper. Almost like cardboard or poster-board material," Hannah remarked.

"Like the kind we used in art class?" Corey asked. "That time we had to make posters?"

"Yeah," Hannah said, nodding.

"Wait a minute," said Ben, looking away from the monitor. "That guy protesting at the rally was a retired art teacher."

"Mr. Powell," Corey said.

"Right. And I think the sign he was carrying was on poster board."

Hannah looked doubtful. "I'm not sure that proves much. You can get white poster board just about anywhere."

Ben started tapping his computer's keyboard. "I'm not saying it proves anything. I'm just saying it might be worth talking to Mr. Powell. Ah, here's his address."

Corey said, "He was probably teaching twenty-five years ago when the Rocky the Ram costume was destroyed. Maybe that gave him the idea."

"But why would he do it?" Hannah asked.

"Possibly to stir up bad feelings between the two teams," Ben suggested. "It could lead them to fight or something, and that might help get football canceled. Then there'd be more money for the arts."

Ben printed out the address, put it into his

pocket, and stood up, ready to go. Corey and Hannah stood up too.

"Okay," Corey said. "I'll go over to Mr. Powell's house. But first I'm gonna need another cookie from your mom."

Mr. Powell's house wasn't big or fancy, but it was nicely taken care of. The front porch had two small statues—one of a giraffe and one of a whale—carved out of wood.

"No ram," Corey observed.

They rang the doorbell. After a moment the door opened. A smiling woman with shoulder-length gray hair stood there. "Yes?" she asked.

"Hello," Hannah said. "Is Mr. Powell here?"

"Yes," she said. "My husband's in his studio. Are you old students of his?" She peered at them closer. "Oh no, you're too young. Well, he'll be happy to see you. He loves young people."

She led them through the house. It was full of artwork—paintings, pottery, mobiles, and more carved statues.

"Your house is like a museum," Corey said.

Mrs. Powell laughed. "A very small one," she replied.

They went through the kitchen and out the door to the backyard. "My husband built his own studio out here, as you can see."

They certainly did see. Much of the backyard was taken up by a one-story wooden building. It was covered in paintings of animals, plants, stones, and people. The roof had several skylights to let the sunshine pour inside.

Mrs. Powell opened the door to the studio. "You have visitors!" she called inside. She turned back to Hannah, Corey, and Ben and gestured for them to come forward. "Go on in."

As soon as they entered the studio, they could smell paint and clay. It reminded Hannah of art class.

"Hello!" Mr. Powell said with a big friendly smile. He was wearing an old blue shirt and jeans. He'd been sitting on a stool in front of a canvas, painting a picture of a panther, based on a photo clipped to the easel. He wiped his hands on a towel. "What can I do for you?"

Ben introduced himself and his two friends. He

said they'd seen him at the pep rally the Friday before and that they were interested in his protest.

"Grow minds, not muscles!" he said with a grin. "You know, I taught art at that high school for thirty-five years. Every year for the last few years, they cut the budget for art and music, until I could barely afford to buy paper and paint for my classes. After I retired, I had the time and freedom to really tell people how I felt about those cuts."

"But why protest at the pep rally?" Corey asked.

"They always seem to have plenty of money for sports," Mr. Powell said. "You should see what they pay the coaches. More than a lot of the teachers."

He picked up a dirty paintbrush and dropped it in a coffee can with a bunch of others. They were soaking in some kind of cleaning fluid.

"Well, sir, with all due respect," Corey said, "it seems to me that your slogan isn't exactly accurate."

Mr. Powell looked surprised. "What do you mean?"

"Football doesn't just grow your muscles," he said. "It grows your mind, too. You have to learn the rules. You have to learn what all the different positions are. You have to memorize complicated plays. And you have to analyze the other team to try to figure out what they're going to do. There's a lot of thinking involved!"

Mr. Powell nodded, impressed. "Well, now, I never quite thought of it that way. Actually, I've got nothing against football players. I just wish the school district would give the arts the funds they need."

"Maybe you need a different slogan," Hannah suggested.

"Maybe you're right," Mr. Powell said, smiling.

"Then you'd have to make a new sign," Ben said. "What do you use?"

"I'll show you." Mr. Powell rummaged through a stack of papers and materials. Eventually he found a piece of white poster board. "If I'm in a hurry, I'll just use a marker. But I prefer to paint the signs with a brush. Any time I can turn a chore into an art project, I'll do it. Just for the fun of it."

Ben picked up the poster board and looked at it. "I've got to get some poster board for a school project. Where do you buy this?"

"There's a terrific art supply store downtown," Mr. Powell said. "They're very helpful, and their prices are fair. I get all my stuff there."

"Did you hear about Rocky the Ram?" Hannah asked.

Mr. Powell looked puzzled. "Who?"

"The school mascot," Hannah explained. "At Woodlands High."

"Oh, right." He shook his head. "No, I didn't hear. What happened?"

"Somebody wrecked the costume," Corey said. "Threw it on the bonfire."

Mr. Powell looked shocked. "That's terrible! Why would anyone do that?"

"I don't know," Hannah said. "But it's happened before. Twenty-five years ago."

Mr. Powell nodded his head slowly. "That's right. I remember that. I was teaching then, and some of the students were really upset. Said they should get back at the guys from the other high school who did it. I don't think they ever did anything, though."

"Where did you say that art supply store is?" Ben asked.

"Downtown," Mr. Powell replied. "I'm surprised you don't know about it. It's been there for years."

"Could you possibly write down the name and address for me?" Ben wondered.

"Sure!" Mr. Powell said agreeably. He found a piece of paper and a pen. Then he wrote down the information and handed the paper to Ben.

"Thanks," Ben said.

After they said good-bye to Mr. Powell and left, Hannah turned to Ben and said, "Handwriting standard?"

Ben nodded.

"Well," Hannah said, "a nonrequested standard is better than a requested standard, but I guess it'll have to do."

She grinned.

Chapter 12

Back in Ben's bedroom, they scanned the piece of paper Mr. Powell had written on. That way, they could zoom in on the document to examine it letter by letter. They could also put it next to the costume destroyer's note on the computer screen, so they could compare the two.

But they didn't actually need all that advanced technology.

Just by glancing at the two pieces of handwriting, they could tell that it was very unlikely the same person had written them both. Mr. Powell's printing was very distinctive. It looked quite different from the writing on the note.

"I kept trying to think of a way to get him to write 'Vikings Rule,' but I couldn't think of one," Ben said.

"It doesn't matter," Hannah said. "It seems obvious that Mr. Powell didn't write that note."

"Unless he disguised his handwriting," Corey noted. "An artist might have really good control of his finger muscles. And we came around asking about Rocky the Ram, so he might have been on to us."

"He didn't seem like someone who would run over a mascot costume and then throw it into a fire," Hannah pointed out. "He seemed really nice."

"Appearances can be deceiving," Corey said. "And his comments about football were not very nice."

"That's true, but I think I agree with Hannah. I'm pretty sure Mr. Powell didn't do it," Ben concluded.

"Yeah, I don't really think he did it either," Corey admitted. "But at least we got to do our first handwriting analysis."

Hannah stared at the computer screen. "You know, I think I can read the personality of the person who wrote down this address."

"Really?" Corey said. "What kind of personality do you see?"

"Artistic," Hannah said, grinning. "And nice."

Ben and Corey laughed.

"You know," Ben said, "when we were talking to Mr. Powell about the incident twenty-five years ago, I started thinking that could be the key to this whole thing."

"How?" Hannah asked.

"I don't know." Ben shook his head. "But it's too big of a coincidence to not be important. I think we need to find out more about what happened back then."

Corey opened a folder on Ben's desk and took out photocopies of the two newspaper articles they'd found at the library. "This is everything the library had. And we checked the Internet. Where are we going to get more information about something that happened twenty-five years ago?"

"Well," Ben said, "Ricky Collins said his dad remembered all about it."

Corey raised his eyebrows.

That night, after they'd gone home to eat dinner, the members of Club CSI met in front of the bakery where Mr. Collins worked.

They stood out in front on the dark sidewalk.

Inside, the bakery was brightly lit. They could smell bread baking.

"How do we even know he'll be here?" Corey asked.

"Well, we don't know for sure," Ben said. "But I heard Ricky say his dad works the night shift. So this seems like a good chance to talk to him without Ricky being around."

They tried opening the front door, but it was locked. "Come on," Ben said. "There must be an employees' entrance around back."

They walked down a narrow gap between the bakery and the building next door. At the back of the building they found a door and then tried the handle. The door opened. The smell of baking bread wafted out into the night air.

Corey took a deep breath. "Mmm," he said. "I wonder if they give free samples."

As they stepped in, a man dressed in white pants, a white shirt, and a white apron walked up to them. He had flour on his hands and arms.

"The shop's closed, kids," he said. "You'll have to come back tomorrow."

"Actually," Hannah said politely, "we were wondering if we might speak with Mr. Collins."

The man looked surprised. "I'm Mr. Collins. How can I help you?"

It was easy to see where Ricky got his size—his dad was a tall, large man. Ricky's face was shaped more like his mother's, though.

"We're in class with your son, Ricky," Corey said.

"And he mentioned you remembered the time twenty-five years ago when Rocky the Ram was destroyed," Ben said.

Mr. Collins nodded. "Yeah, I remember that. What did you want to know?"

"Well, we were wondering . . . ," Hannah began.

But just then the back door opened.

It was Ricky.

"Hey, Dad, I brought your 'lunch,'" he said, holding up a bag. Then he noticed the members of Club CSI. "What are you dorks doing here?!"

"Hi, Ricky," Corey said. "How ya doin'?"

Mr. Collins took the bag. "Ricky, your friends want to hear about the Rocky the Ram thing. The one from twenty-five years ago."

"I'm sure they do," Ricky said. "But Charlie and I are going to win those tickets, not you three." He glared at them.

Club CSI got the message.

"Okay, I guess we'll just see you at school," Ben said, heading toward the door. "Thanks, anyway, Mr. Collins."

"Thanks?" he asked. "What for? I didn't tell you anything."

Ben was already outside. Hannah followed him out. As he reached the door, Corey turned back.

"You don't give out free bread samples, do you?"

Chapter 13

The next day the three members of Club CSI were feeling a little discouraged. Ricky had stopped his dad before he'd told them anything about the destruction of Rocky the Ram twenty-five years ago, so the whole trip to the bakery had been a waste of time.

"We didn't even get any free samples," Corey muttered.

"I was thinking," Hannah said. "Maybe instead of trying to find out exactly what happened twenty-five years ago, we should check out what happened one year ago."

"What do you mean?" Ben asked.

"Remember what those football players said? About Steve?" she said.

"The guy who wears the Viking costume for Jefferson High?" Corey asked.

"They said he got into a fight with Mitchell," Ben remembered.

"That's right," Hannah said. "Maybe we should go talk to Steve."

"Find out if he has a car," Corey added.

"Get a handwriting standard," Ben said.

"Nonrequested, if possible," Hannah reminded them.

Right after school that day, the three friends walked up the sidewalk toward a house. A quick Internet search had given them Steve's last name. . . . All they'd had to do was enter "Current Viking mascot, Jefferson High School, Nevada," and his name came up in an article from the high school paper. Luckily, he had an unusual last name, so they were also able to find his address.

They had their story ready.

Hannah rang the doorbell. A blond guy opened the door. He looked the right age.

"Hi!" Hannah said cheerfully. "Are you Steve?"

"Yes," he said a little suspiciously. He wondered if they were going to try to get him to buy something or contribute to their organization.

"Steve the Jefferson High Viking?" Corey asked.

He nodded.

"We're doing an article on mascots for our journalism class," Ben said. "We wondered if we could ask you some questions."

Steve smiled. "Sure!" he said. "Come on in!"

They all sat down in the living room. Steve even offered them water or soda. They politely said "no, thanks" since they already felt a little guilty about pretending to be working on a school assignment. Well, actually they *were* working on a school assignment. It just wasn't in journalism.

"Do you mind if we record this?" Hannah asked, getting out her phone. She figured journalists probably recorded their interviews.

"Not at all," Steve said, smiling again. He seemed excited to be the subject of a real interview, even if it was just for a junior high school class.

"So, how did you become the Viking mascot?" Ben asked.

Steve told them all about auditioning for the

mascot and how excited he was when he'd found out he'd been picked.

"You really like being the Viking?" Corey asked.

"I love it!" Steve said. "It's great! I love going to all the games and the rallies and getting the crowd going so they're really into it."

"Do you ever get together with any of the other mascots?" Hannah asked.

Steve looked confused. "You mean, like, away from the games? Out of costume?"

"Yeah," Hannah said.

"No," Steve said. "That would be kind of weird."

"Do you know Mitchell?" Ben asked. "The guy who does Rocky the Ram?"

Steve frowned. "Yeah, I know him."

"What's the matter?" Hannah asked. "Is he not a good mascot?"

Steve hesitated. "Well, I don't want to say anything bad about a fellow mascot. Especially if you're going to put it in your article."

Corey shook his head. "This part can be totally off the record. We were thinking about interviewing Mitchell. But then we talked to someone who thought Mitchell wasn't dedicated to being a mascot."

Steve nodded. "They're right. Mitchell's not dedicated. I've seen him at games in full costume, taking off the head to talk to the cheerleaders. Like he's not Rocky the Ram at all. He's just some guy in a costume. And this is *during the game*. Where everyone can see him. Really inappropriate. I mean, to me, the mascot costume is sacred."

"Did you ever say something to him about it?" Ben asked.

"Yeah, I did," Steve said. "After the game. He didn't appreciate my comments."

"You fought?" Corey asked.

"No!" Steve said, surprised. "Who told you that?"

Corey shrugged. "I protect my sources."

"It wasn't a fight," Steve insisted. "We may have . . . pushed each other a couple of times. That's all."

"Did you hear about what happened to the Rocky the Ram costume?" Ben asked.

Steve stood up. "Yeah, that was terrible. Listen, I'm going to get some water. You sure you don't want anything?"

Hannah, Ben, and Corey stood up too. "No,"

Hannah said. "Actually, I think we've got all the info we need."

"Really?" Steve asked. "That's it?"

"It's a short assignment," Corey said.

"Oh, but that reminds me," Ben said. "Our teacher wanted proof of our interviews."

"Wow, she sounds tough," Steve said, smiling. "Well, you've got your recording."

Ben had forgotten Hannah had recorded the interview.

"Right," he said slowly, "but the teacher doesn't want to listen to all those interviews, so she asked us to get something written from each of our sources."

"Like what?" Steve asked, puzzled.

Ben handed him a pad of paper and a pen. "If you could just write, 'I gave an interview to Ben, Corey, and Hannah. They have my permission to use this interview to write an article for their journalism class.' Then sign your name."

"Whoa, slow down," Steve said. "Say that again."

As Steve wrote, Ben slowly repeated what he'd said, as best as he could remember it.

The Viking finished, capped the pen, and handed it and the pad back to Ben. "Is that all you need?"

Ben smiled. "That should do it. Thanks."

As they walked out the front door, Hannah pointed to a car parked out in the street. "Is that your car?"

"No, mine's parked in back," Steve said.

"You have your own car?" Corey said. "Cool."

Steve laughed. "Yeah, well, it's just an old beater."

"Still," Corey said, "a car's a car."

Back in Ben's bedroom, Club CSI scanned the handwriting standard they'd gotten from Steve.

"I've gotta say, I really doubt Steve drove over Rocky the Ram and then threw him on the bonfire," Corey said, bouncing his tennis ball against the wall and catching it. Ben watched him nervously.

"Please don't do that in here," Ben said. "Something could break. My microscopes, my computer . . ."

"I won't miss," Corey said. "I'm very good at throwing this ball and catching it."

"I know you don't *plan* to miss, but it's still within the realm of possibility," Ben said.

"Fine." Corey sighed, shoving the ball into his backpack.

"Why do you doubt Steve destroyed the costume?" Hannah asked. "He obviously doesn't like Mitchell and probably wouldn't mind getting him in trouble."

"Yeah, but you heard what he said," Corey said. "To him, a mascot costume is *sacred*!"

"True," Hannah admitted.

"Let's compare his handwriting standard with the note before we make up our minds," Ben said.

They stared at the computer screen.

"Look at his *r*'s," Hannah said. "He prints them like they're capital *r*'s, even when they're in the middle of a word. Whoever wrote the note didn't do that. See the *r* in 'ready'?"

"You're right," Ben said. "And I watched him while he was writing for us. He's left-handed. Remember what Miss Hodges told us about clues that can help an investigator tell if a person is right- or left-handed? That's why the bars across his *t*'s are heavier on the right side and thinner on the left side."

"Yeah," Corey said. "But in the note, it's the

opposite. The bar across the *t* is lighter on the right side and heavier on the left."

"So whoever wrote the note is right-handed," Hannah said.

"It's not a match," Ben concluded. "Steve didn't write the note."

"I knew it," Corey said.

They sat there for a minute, thinking.

"So, what else have we got?" Hannah asked.

"There's the tire track," Corey said. "The one we saw on the costume. Maybe we could do something with that."

"Like what?" Hannah asked.

"I don't know," Corey admitted. "But I know who does. Maybe she's still at school."

"Tire tracks?" Miss Hodges asked. She was just about to leave for the weekend when Club CSI burst into her classroom. "We won't get to that unit for another month."

"Couldn't you give us a sneak preview?" Corey asked.

"Well," she said, crossing to the dry-erase board,

"do you remember the difference between class evidence and individual evidence?"

She wrote "class" and "individual" on the board.

"Class evidence helps you put an object in a group of objects, like a brand," Ben answered. "Individual evidence helps you identify one specific object."

"That's right," Miss Hodges said. "In the case of tire marks, you're much more likely to get class evidence than individual evidence."

"So the tire mark could tell you what brand of tire it came from, but it might not lead you to one specific tire on one specific car," Hannah said.

"Exactly," Miss Hodges. "As for the specifics of analyzing tire marks, I'd recommend talking to a tire expert."

"Do you know any tire experts?" Hannah asked.

Miss Hodges looked out the classroom window. "Not here in town. I know one in Las Vegas, but that's not real handy."

"There's a tire store on Prospect Avenue," Ben said. "My dad buys his tires there. He complains about their prices, but he says they know what they're doing."

The teacher smiled. "Sounds like a good place to try."

The young guy behind the counter grinned. "Expert? Well, I guess we're all tire experts here. But the man you should talk to is Bob. He's been working with tires since before you were born. Heck, before *I* was born!"

Hannah returned the guy's smile. Bob sounded perfect. "Is he here?"

"Yep," the young guy said. "He's in the garage. Follow me."

They went past a glass door and into the area where customers brought their cars to have their tires changed. Early this Saturday morning, it was quiet, with no cars and no customers.

At the back of the garage an older man was running his finger along the tires on a rack. He seemed to be checking to see which tires they had in stock.

"Hey, Bob!" the younger man called. "Got some young folks here who are looking for a tire expert."

"Well," Bob said. "If I see one, I'll let you know."

The younger man chuckled. "No one knows more about tires than you, Bob."

"I doubt that," Bob said good-naturedly. "But I'll be glad to help any way I can. What do you need? Bicycle tires? 'Cause we don't sell those."

"We need to learn about car tires for a school project," Hannah said.

Bob puffed out his cheeks. "Car tires. That's a big subject. It seems like the more I learn about them, the more I realize how little I know."

He walked across the garage toward a poster showing a tire cut in half, so customers could see all the pieces that went into making one. He talked as he walked. Club CSI followed him, with Ben taking notes on a small pad.

"Every year, there are more than a billion new tires made. Lots of companies make them. They come in all sizes, but not all shapes. They're all round." He winked.

When he reached the poster, Bob pointed to the different parts of the tire as he described them.

"There are two main parts to a tire: the body and the tread. The body is for support—to hold the car up. The tread is for traction—to grip the road."

He pointed to the center hole of the tire. "The part of the tire right next to the rim is called the bead. Between the bead and the tread is the sidewall. This edge between the sidewall and the beginning of the tread is the shoulder."

Ben said, "It's mostly the tread we're interested in. We're trying to identify a tire print."

Hannah showed Bob the picture on her phone of the tire print. "This is the tire print we're trying to identify."

Bob raised his glasses and looked at the phone closely. "What's the tire print on? Doesn't look like pavement. Almost looks . . . hairy."

"It's a mascot costume," Corey explained. "Rocky the Ram."

Bob looked at Corey with raised eyebrows. "This sounds like a very interesting school project."

"Can you tell what kind of tire might have left that print?" Ben asked.

"Hmm," Bob said, staring at the picture. "It's tricky. I'm trying to see the pattern from the lugs, the grooves, and the sipes."

"The whats?" Corey asked.

Bob grinned. "Here, I'll show you." He walked

over to a rack full of tires and then knelt down next to one of them.

"The lugs are these kind of square-shaped bits of rubber that touch the road when you drive. They also make the marks in a tire print," he explained.

He ran his finger along a channel that ran around the tire. "This is a groove. In the tire print, these look like spaces between the marks made by the lugs."

He flicked his fingernail into little cuts that were angled across the lugs. "These little cuts are called sipes. They're actually named after the guy who invented them, John F. Sipes. Legend has it that he cut slits in the soles of his shoes to keep from slipping at work. I'm not sure whether I believe that."

"What are they for?" Corey asked.

"They help get water off your tire, so you won't slip. The spaces in a tire also give the lug somewhere to expand when the weight of the car is on it. They help reduce heating and even tire noise."

He stood up. "So every tire designer has his theories about the best combination and pattern of lugs, grooves, and sipes to give you the best traction and durability."

Hannah held up her phone with the tire print picture on it. "And what can you tell us about the tire that made this print?"

Bob peered at the picture again. "It's hard to say. For one thing, there's nothing in the picture to tell me what size the print is."

Hannah silently chided herself for not thinking of that when she took the picture. She should have put a ruler next to the tire print before snapping the photo. Next time . . .

"But it looks like a fairly ordinary car tire," he continued. "Nothing special. Not a high-performance tire, or a mud and snow tire. If I had to guess the brand, I'd say . . . Acme Value Tires. But that's just a guess."

He waved a hand toward the hundreds of tires in the store. "You're welcome to look at our tires and see if you can find a match." He grinned. "Might take a while, though."

"No, thank you," Ben said. "But that's a good idea. We have a few specific cars we could check to see if they match."

Chapter 15

Hannah was nervous. When she'd agreed to take pictures of Steve's tires on Sunday afternoon, it had seemed like it would be easy. But now as she approached his house, she felt butterflies in her stomach.

Why were they bothering to take pictures of Steve's tires, anyway? Hadn't they agreed that the Viking's handwriting standard didn't match the note? That the note was written by someone who was right-handed and that Steve was left-handed?

Ben and Corey had thought they needed to be thorough. Corey called it "covering all the bases." Ben had called it "gathering as much evidence as possible." Hannah was starting to think of it as "a scary waste of time."

Steve had said his car wasn't parked in front of the house along the street. He'd said it was parked in back. She hoped that was where he always parked it. If it was parked out front, she wouldn't know which one it was.

Hannah couldn't cut through the yard. Someone might see her through a window. And that would be bad.

She walked around the block to the alley. She'd noticed that Steve's house was the fourth house from the end. She walked up the alley to the fourth house, trying to look casual. Her cell phone was in her hand.

What if the car was locked in a garage? But she was in luck. There was a carport with two cars parked under it. One was shiny and new. The other was old and dented. Steve had called his car a "beater."

She ducked down behind the car. Snapped pictures of both back tires with her camera. Got up and walked quickly away before anyone noticed.

Mission accomplished.

Corey had no problem taking pictures of Mr. Powell's tires. His car was parked behind his studio. Mr. and Mrs. Powell were nowhere around. He was probably in his studio, and she was probably in the house. Easy.

But now he was looking for Mitchell's house. Ben had found the address and written it down for him. Corey was walking along an unfamiliar street, checking the addresses, looking for number 514 . . .

He didn't even know if Mitchell had a car. When they'd talked to Mitchell, they hadn't been focusing on the tire print yet. So they hadn't asked Mitchell whether or not he had a car.

Corey figured he'd just go to the house, find the cars, and take pictures of all their tires with his camera, which took much better pictures than his phone.

That reminded him. He'd love to get a new phone.

Focus! He went back to scanning the house numbers. Aha! There it was! Number 514!

Luckily, there weren't any cars parked on the street out front, so he wouldn't have to take pictures of all of them.

But he would have to go behind the house. It

was in the middle of the block. He didn't really want to walk all the way around.

He quickly slipped through the neighbor's yard. No one yelled at him. So far, so good.

Corey found an open garage with two cars parked inside. He ducked down and started taking pictures of the tires with his camera.

But then he heard the back door of the house open and close.

Not knowing where to hide, he slid under one of the cars.

He heard someone entering the garage. If they got in the car, he'd have to crawl out before they started the engine. They'd be sure to see him. That would be very awkward.

He saw a pair of legs walk back and forth and then pause in midstride, as if the person attached to the legs was looking for something. Corey's imagination began to run wild as he wondered what he would do if the person stayed in the garage for a long time. How long could he stay hidden under a car? Finally, after what seemed like an eternity but was really just a few moments, the legs started moving again, and the person headed toward a garbage container.

From his vantage point, Corey could see that the legs wore women's pants and gym shoes.

Corey heard the garbage container open. *Whoompf!* The person dropped a trash bag into the container. *Bam!* The lid to the container dropped back down.

The feet walked out of the garage. And back into the house.

Corey breathed a huge sigh of relief. He finished taking pictures of the two cars' tires and then got out of there as fast as he could, brushing dirt off his clothes as he ran.

Ben thought his assignment was the hardest: taking pictures of cars parked at Jefferson High School.

But somehow it didn't seem right for Hannah to do it. And he understood why Corey didn't want to get in trouble with football players since he was a football player himself.

Of course, Ben didn't want to get in trouble with football players, either.

There weren't too many cars in the parking lot today. Ben hoped most of them belonged to the football players, who were there for practice on this weekend afternoon.

As he snapped pictures of the cars' tires, he thought he probably should have come up with some sort of explanation to cover why he was doing this, just in case somebody—

"Hey, what are you doing?"

He looked up and saw a high school kid staring at him.

"Oh, just taking some pictures," Ben said.

"Of what?" the kid asked.

"Tires," Ben answered honestly.

"Why?" the kid persisted.

This was the moment when it would have been nice if Ben had thought of a good cover story.

He just stood there for a moment.

Then he blurted out, "For the yearbook."

"Oh," said the kid, completely satisfied with this answer. "Cool."

In Ben's bedroom, Club CSI started to compare their photos of tires with the picture of the tire print from the Rocky the Ram costume.

"Why are you so dirty?" Hannah said to Corey. "I mean, even more than usual."

"Because Mitchell needs to clean his family's garage," Corey replied, brushing off more dirt.

"Hey!" Ben said. "You're brushing that dirt right onto my bed!"

"Sorry," said Corey. He picked up a wastebasket and tried to sweep the dirt from his clothes into it with his hand. Most of it went on the floor. "Um . . . got a broom?"

"Forget it," Ben said. "We've got a lot of pictures to compare. We should get going on them."

They settled down to the incredibly tedious business of staring at photos of tires. At first they all looked the same. But the more pictures they stared at, the more familiar they became with the patterns of the treads. What were the words Bob had used? The lugs. The grooves. The sipes. They kind of sounded like names for weird bands. Soon the three friends could quickly eliminate a photo as not matching the print from the costume.

In the end, none of the pictures matched perfectly.

"But this one seems to be the closest," Hannah

said, holding up one of the photos they'd printed out on Ben's printer.

"Which one is it?" Ben asked.

Hannah turned the picture over to read the label they'd scrawled on the back. "It's one of the cars in Mitchell's garage," she said.

All three looked at one another, thinking.

"We should talk to Mitchell again," Ben suggested.

"I know where his house is," Corey said.

Chapter 16

After school on Monday, Club CSI went back to Woodlands High School to see if they could find Mitchell and talk to him.

They walked right by the site of the bonfire, so they paused to see if they might spot anything new or different. But the custodians had done a good job of cleaning up. There was no sign the bonfire had ever been there.

As they walked across the parking lot, Corey looked around for Mitchell's car. "Maybe you'd recognize it better if you crawled underneath," Hannah teased.

"Very funny," Corey said. "I'm pretty sure I'll know it when I see it."

Suddenly he pointed.

"There it is!" he cried. Ben and Hannah looked to see where he was pointing and saw a small blue car—nothing fancy.

"Just out of curiosity," Ben said, "let's see what kind of tires Mitchell has."

They walked over to the car. After looking around to see if anyone was watching, they knelt down to check the tires.

"It should have the brand name on the sidewall," Ben said.

"'Sidewall,'" Hannah said. "Excellent use of tire vocabulary."

"Thank you," he said with a slight bow of his head.

It was an overcast afternoon, and the name of the company that made the tires was the same color as the tire—black on black. So the brand name wasn't obvious.

But then Corey spotted it. The way the tire was positioned, he had to turn his head upside down to read it. "Acme Value Tires," he said.

"Score one for Bob," Hannah said.

"Excuse me," said a voice above them. "What are you doing?"

They looked up and saw Mitchell looking down at them. He did not look happy.

"Oh sorry," Corey said. "We were settling a bet."

"A bet? About what?"

"Well, Ben has this thing he always claims he can do," Corey explained, making it up as he went along. "He says he can tell what brand a tire is just by looking at it. So we were checking to see what brand the tires are on this car."

"Why? Is it your car?" Hannah asked innocently.

"Yeah," Mitchell said. "It's my parents'. They let me use it."

Ben, Hannah, and Corey stood up. They stayed there by Mitchell's car, blocking his way to the driver's side door.

"Excuse me," he said. "I've got to get home."

"We were wondering if we could ask you some more questions about Rocky the Ram," Ben said.

"Sorry," Mitchell said. "Now's not a good time. I've got a ton of homework and a test in algebra tomorrow. I've got to get home to study."

"Oh," Ben said. "Okay."

They stepped out of Mitchell's way. He started to open the door.

"Um, would you mind giving me your e-mail address so we could just shoot you an e-mail with our questions?" Ben asked.

Mitchell paused. "Well, I couldn't answer your e-mail tonight. Like I said, I've got homework and studying to do."

Ben smiled his friendliest smile. "No, you wouldn't have to answer any questions tonight. But if you wouldn't mind giving me your e-mail address now, then we'd have it."

Mitchell sighed. "All right. You can type it into your phone."

Hannah got out her phone. But Ben said, "I thought your phone was out of charge, Hannah."

Hannah stood there for a second. "Oh yeah," she said. "That's right. I forgot to charge it up."

"That's okay," Ben said. He reached into his backpack. "Here. I've got a pad and a pen." He pulled them out and offered them to Mitchell. "If you could just write down your e-mail address, and maybe when the best time for you to answer our questions might be . . ."

But Mitchell was already getting in his car. "My phone number is listed online."

"Um, yeah, but—"

"Then just call me if you have any questions," he said. "But don't call tonight." He slammed his door shut, started the car, and backed out of his parking space. Then he peeled out of the parking lot.

Club CSI watched him go.

"That was weird," Hannah said.

"I was just trying to get him to write down his e-mail address so we could have a writing standard to compare to the costume wrecker's note," Ben explained. "I realize it would've been a requested standard, but I didn't see any way we could get a nonrequested standard."

"I knew what you were doing," Hannah said. "I meant Mitchell's behavior was really weird."

"Yeah," Corey agreed. "What's the big deal with writing down your e-mail address? It's almost like he knew you were just trying to get a sample of his handwriting to compare to the note."

"At this point, Mitchell is definitely suspect number one," Hannah said.

"I'm starting to think those VIP football tickets are as good as mine," Corey said. "I mean, ours."

"We still need a handwriting standard from

Mitchell," Ben said. "But I'm inclined to agree with you."

Club CSI was feeling confident that they had cracked the case.

That's why the next day at school was such a surprise. . . .

Chapter 17

"C lass, I have an announcement," Miss Hodges said at the beginning of forensic science. "The Rocky the Ram mystery has been solved!"

Hannah, Ben, and Corey looked at one another, shocked. They were pretty sure Mitchell had ruined the costume, but they still needed more evidence, so they hadn't said anything to Miss Hodges yet.

And now she was announcing that the case was closed.

"There go my VIP tickets," Corey murmured. He didn't even bother to correct himself and say "our VIP tickets." The contest was over, and they'd lost.

"Who did it?" Jennifer asked eagerly.

"And who solved it?" Kayla added.

"There's been a confession," Miss Hodges said. "Another note was left pinned to the tree at the high school."

She held up a piece of white poster board. "It says, 'We burned Rocky. We're sorry. GO VIKINGS!—The Vikings Football Team.'"

Miss Hodges set the note down on the front table. "So the football players at Jefferson High School committed the arson."

Ricky Collins's hand shot into the air. "Miss Hodges?" he said. "You forgot to mention that it was our team that found the note—me and Charlie. So we won the contest, right?"

Hannah spun around in her seat to face Ricky. "Finding a confession isn't solving a mystery. You didn't use forensic science. You just got lucky!"

"Sometimes luck is what makes all the difference in solving a case," Ricky said. "Right, Miss Hodges?"

"Sometimes," Miss Hodges admitted. "As for whether you actually won the contest, I'm still debating that issue."

"It wasn't just luck," Charlie said. "We found the note because we were at the high school

investigating. We wanted to check out the crime scene again."

Ben thought to himself that Charlie and Ricky had definitely provided some tough competition to Club CSI.

"Plus, we *did* use forensic science," Charlie continued. "Before we turned the new note over to Miss Hodges, we used handwriting analysis to see if it matched the old note."

"And did it match?" Corey asked.

Charlie smiled, nodding. "It sure did. The results were conclusive."

Ben silently disagreed. He didn't believe the investigation had come to its full conclusion. "Has the football team been questioned?" he asked.

"I told Principal Inverno about the new note first thing this morning," Miss Hodges said. "And he called Principal Hall at Woodlands High School. Principal Hall communicated with the principal at Jefferson High School immediately. All three principals are convinced that the football team burned Rocky the Ram, so the team members will be held responsible."

"That was always the rumor," Ryan said. "That the Vikings did it."

"But rumors aren't facts!" Corey protested, even though he himself had thought for quite a while that the Vikings had destroyed the costume.

"Maybe not," Ricky said. "But it's a fact that my partner and I found a signed confession. Case closed. I'll wave to you from my VIP seat at the games, losers!"

Miss Hodges repeated that she hadn't yet made up her mind about whether Ricky and Charlie had won. She set the matter aside and began the day's lesson in forensic science.

After class, Hannah, Corey, and Ben stuck around to talk to Miss Hodges. She was putting away the materials the students had used in that day's activities.

"Miss Hodges, we were wondering if you could do us a small favor," Hannah said.

"Sure," the teacher replied brightly. "What is it?"

"Could you ask that tire expert you know in Las Vegas to compare two pictures of tire marks for us?" Hannah asked. "We could e-mail the photos to him."

Miss Hodges stopped putting materials away. She looked confused. "Tire marks?" she asked. "Weren't those part of your Rocky the Ram investigation?

That case is closed. Why would you want a tire expert to look at your photos now that the case is over?"

The three friends hesitated to answer her. They didn't want to accuse her, and the three principals, and their classmates of getting the solution wrong without stronger evidence against Mitchell. All they really had was some fishy behavior and a blurry tire print.

"Oh, that's okay, Miss Hodges," Corey said. "Forget it."

"Yeah, never mind," Ben added.

Miss Hodges smiled gently. "The case has been solved, but there's no need for you three to feel frustrated by that. You did the best you could. Just because you didn't solve the case doesn't mean you're not great investigators. You'll get 'em next time."

The three friends looked at one another. Miss Hodges thought they were sore losers! She totally had the wrong idea! Now they definitely had to prove Mitchell had destroyed Rocky the Ram. But they'd have to do it without Miss Hodges's Las Vegas expert.

"Okay, Miss Hodges," Hannah said, smiling. "Thanks. See you tomorrow."

As they walked down the school hallway, they thought about what they could possibly do next. "We really need that handwriting standard from Mitchell," Ben said. "I'm guessing it'll match the original note *and* the new note."

They kept walking, trying to think of a way to get Mitchell to write something for them. Send him a present and hope he'd write them a thank-you note?

Then Corey thought of something.

"I wonder if Ricky and Charlie ever got a handwriting sample from Mitchell. Charlie definitely thought of using handwriting analysis to solve the case. He used it to match the two notes to each other."

"Are you saying we should go ask Ricky and Charlie for a sample of Mitchell's handwriting?" Hannah asked.

"Well," Corey said, "we could just ask Charlie."

Chapter 18

At lunch, they found Charlie in the cafeteria. He was sitting by himself, eating a sandwich.

"Hi, Charlie," Hannah said cheerfully. "How's your lunch?"

"It's okay, I guess," he said. "Just a sandwich."

"We were wondering if maybe we could ask you something about your investigation of Rocky the Ram," Corey said.

Charlie thought for a second. Then he said, "I don't know. I'd have to consult with my partner."

"Partner?" Corey said. "Oh, you mean Ricky?"

"Where is he?" Ben asked.

"Right over there," Charlie said, looking toward the back corner of the cafeteria.

Ricky was sitting with his old friends from the

back of the classroom. They were laughing and stealing one another's food.

"Fine," Hannah said. "Consult away."

Charlie got up and walked over to Ricky's table. Club CSI watched as he talked to Ricky, who looked over at them. He rolled his eyes, shaking his head. Charlie said something else to Ricky. Finally, he sighed, stood up, and walked over to Corey, Ben, and Hannah. Charlie followed Ricky, walking just behind him.

Ricky stood in front of them, his arms folded across his chest. "Charlie says you want to ask us something about our investigation. I told him you're just jealous we solved the case, so now you're trying to poke holes in our discoveries."

"'Discoveries'? You found a note pinned to a tree," Corey said.

"We're not trying to poke any holes," Ben said. "We're just working on a theory of our own."

"Why?" Ricky asked. "The case is solved. The Vikings did it."

"When you were doing your investigation," Hannah said, trying to smooth things over, "did you happen to get a sample of Mitchell's handwriting?"

"Again, I've got to ask why?" Ricky said. "Why would you need a sample from the guy who wore the costume when we know the football players did it?"

"I'll show you," Ben said. He sat down at the table and opened his backpack. He took out a folder labeled "Tire Prints." From the folder he took two pieces of paper and laid them side by side on the table. Then he motioned for Charlie and Ricky to sit down.

Charlie looked at Ricky to see what he was going to do. Ricky rolled his eyes again, but he unfolded his arms and plopped down in a chair. Charlie sat down too. So did Hannah and Corey.

Ben pushed the two pieces of paper toward Ricky and Charlie. They looked down at them, puzzled.

"What am I looking at?" Ricky said.

Charlie touched one of the pieces of paper. "This one looks like a picture of the ram costume." He touched the other paper. "And this one looks like a close-up of a tire."

"That's exactly right, Charlie," Ben said. "We found bits of dirt, glass, and stone in that spot on the costume."

"The kind of things you'd find in the grooves of a tire," Corey said.

"So we looked at the picture closely, and we realized we were looking at a car's tire print," Hannah said.

Charlie looked closely and then nodded. "You're right. That's a good catch. I should have seen that."

Ricky frowned. He looked confused. "Wait. So you're saying the football players ran over the costume with a car before they threw Rocky on the bonfire?"

"Not exactly," Ben said. He lowered his voice. He didn't want other kids in the cafeteria overhearing his accusation before he had better proof.

"I'm saying *Mitchell* drove over the costume before he threw Rocky on the bonfire."

"Why Mitchell?" Charlie asked.

"Because the other picture is of a tire on Mitchell's car," Corey explained. "And it matches the tire print from the costume. We think."

Ricky stared at the two pictures. Then he shook his head. "Maybe," he said. "I don't know, though. They're not exactly alike."

"It's tough to get a good, clear tire print from a

hairy mascot costume," Hannah pointed out.

"Plus," Ben said, "whoever wrote the notes is right-handed. And Mitchell is right-handed."

Ricky snorted. "So are lots of people! *I'm* right-handed! You think I wrote the notes?"

"It's not just the tire print and the fact that Mitchell's right-handed," Ben said. "It's also the way he acted when we talked to him and tried to get a writing sample from him. But we need harder proof. We really need that writing sample."

"Did you happen to get a writing sample from Mitchell when you were doing your investigation?" Hannah asked.

Ricky and Charlie shook their heads. "No, we didn't," Charlie said. "I should have thought of that too."

"He probably wouldn't have given you one, anyway," Corey said. "He wouldn't even write down his e-mail address for us."

Ricky was thinking. Suddenly he snapped his fingers. *Snap!*

"I got it," he said. "The sign-in sheet at the gym."

Ben started nodding and smiling. "You're right! That's a great idea!"

Corey looked confused. "Um, I'm lost," he said.

"Mitchell had to go into the gym all the time to put on the mascot costume," Ben explained. "Every time he went in, he had to sign in. If we can get a copy of those sign-in sheets, we'll have a sample of his handwriting."

"A nonrequested standard," Charlie said.

"Perfect!" Hannah said. "We'll go over to the gym after school to see if they'll let us have copies of the sign-in sheets."

The three friends started to make a plan, but Ricky put up his palm and whistled loudly to stop their conversation.

They looked at him.

"No," he said. "It was my idea. If anyone's going to the gym, it's me and Charlie."

"Why?" Corey asked. "I thought you said the case was solved."

"Fine," Ricky said firmly. "We'll *all* go."

Chapter 19

The two teams met after school and walked to the high school together. Once they got to Woodlands High, they found the same assistant coach who had shown Club CSI the room where the mascot costume had been stored.

"What brings you back here?" he asked. "I heard the case was solved. The players over at Jefferson did it."

"Yes, we heard that too," Hannah said. "But we wanted to tie up a few loose ends."

The assistant coach shrugged. "Well, okay. How can I help?"

"You know the sign-in sheets by the front door to the gym?" Ben asked.

The coach nodded. "Sure."

"Do you happen to keep those?" Ben asked. "Going back to, say, the beginning of the school year?"

"You know, I don't actually know the answer to that question," he said frankly. "But we can find out. Follow me."

He led them out of the gym and into the high school's main building. They walked down a long hallway to the main office.

"Mary," he said to the woman behind the counter, "these fine young students from the junior high were wondering if we keep the sign-in sheets from the gym."

She smiled. "We certainly do."

"May we look at them, please?" Charlie asked politely.

"I don't see why not," Mary said, turning toward a filing cabinet. She found a folder full of sign-in sheets and handed it to Charlie.

It didn't take the five investigators long to find several sheets with Mitchell's name written on them. "May we have photocopies of these sheets?" Hannah asked. "We could pay for the seven copies."

Mary laughed. "That's all right. I think we can

afford seven copies for you." She quickly made the copies and handed them to Hannah.

"Thank you so much," she said.

Outside, they wasted no time in comparing the sign-in sheets to Hannah's picture of the first note.

"A magnifying glass would help," Charlie said.

Ben pulled two from his backpack. Charlie grinned. "You came prepared."

They carefully compared the letters in Mitchell's name to those letters as they appeared in the note. They paid attention to the way each letter was formed.

It was a match.

"I wish we had a copy of the second note," Corey said. "I know the two notes matched, but I'd like to compare the new note to Mitchell's sign-in."

"Here," Charlie said, handing Corey his phone. "When we found the new note, I took a picture of it with my cell."

"All right!" Corey said, sliding his fingers across the screen to enlarge the picture of the note.

That one matched the writing on the sign-in sheets, too.

"Okay, I'll admit it," Ricky said finally. "Looks like Mitchell's our man."

When they showed the matching writing to Miss Hodges, she was impressed. "Very good analysis," she said. "I'm particularly impressed by how your two teams worked together."

Hannah tried to keep from smiling. She was remembering how hard they'd worked at the beginning to keep Ricky from overhearing their plans.

Ben showed Miss Hodges the picture of the tire print and the picture of Mitchell's tire. "If we need more evidence, maybe your expert in Las Vegas could see whether these really do match."

"Definitely," Miss Hodges said.

As it turned out, they didn't need the opinion of Miss Hodges's tire expert after all.

When they confronted Mitchell with the evidence in Principal Hall's office, he made a full confession.

"It was an accident," he said. "I didn't mean to ruin the costume."

"So you accidentally ran over it and then threw it on the bonfire?" Ricky asked sarcastically.

"Just tell us what happened, Mitchell," Hannah said. "It'll be okay."

He sighed. "It was at the away game against Farrow High. After the game I was walking back to my car wearing the costume. I had the head off. As I was about to put the head into the trunk, one of the cheerleaders came up and started talking to me."

He blushed. Corey nodded, remembering what Mitchell had said before about wanting to meet the cheerleaders.

"My trunk latch sticks, and I didn't want to struggle with it in front of her, so I just set the head down on the ground while I talked to her. We talked for a while, and I was feeling really happy, and I totally forgot about the head."

"You backed over it," Ben concluded.

Mitchell nodded sadly. "Yeah. I heard it crunch. I stopped immediately, but it was too late. The head was flattened. I knew how expensive the costume was, and I was afraid I'd get in major trouble. Luckily, no one had seen me drive over the head."

"So you decided to sneak the costume into the bonfire and then write a note that would make everyone think the Vikings did it, just like twenty-five years ago," Charlie said.

"Yeah," Mitchell admitted. "That's right. Then you guys started asking all these questions and poking around my car. I thought the second note would put an end to it."

Mitchell looked at Principal Hall. "Am I going to jail?" he asked.

"No," Principal Hall said sternly. "But you're going to work to pay back the school for the costume."

Relieved, Mitchell blew out a chest full of air. "That's fair," he said.

As the five investigators walked out of the high school together, Corey said, "You know, I just thought of something. Mitchell burned the costume to cover up running over the head. What's that word for when you destroy evidence to hide a crime?"

"Spoliation," Ben and Charlie said at the same time.

"Right!" Corey said. "Isn't that what I suggested in the beginning?"

Miss Hodges made an announcement in class the next day. "I've decided that both teams will receive extra credit. They solved this mystery together."

Then she picked up an envelope. "And here are the VIP tickets to the football games. Two of you will be sitting together."

Hannah, Ben, and Charlie weren't interested in the football games.

That left Corey and Ricky.

Corey looked at Ricky. "I guess I'll see you at the games, partner."

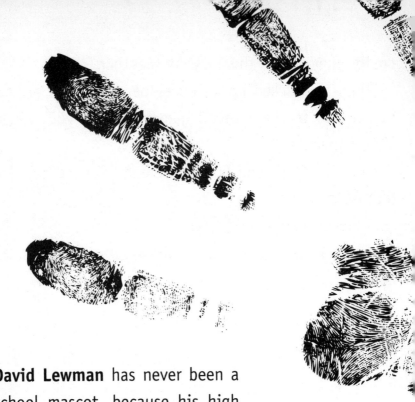

David Lewman has never been a school mascot, because his high school didn't have a football team, but he did play drums in the school band. He has written more than sixty-five books starring SpongeBob SquarePants, Jimmy Neutron, the Fairly OddParents, G.I. Joe, the Wild Thornberrys, and other popular characters. He has also written scripts for many acclaimed television shows. David lives in Los Angeles with his wife, Donna, and their dog, Pirkle.